AF416041

ALSO BY TABITHA O'CONNELL

Structural Integrity
Structural Strain

Dirt-Stained Hands, Thorn-Pierced Skin

TABITHA O'CONNELL

Dirt-Stained
Hands,
Thorn-Pierced
Skin

CONTENT NOTE

This book contains:

- Minor injury & blood
- Mild body horror
- Reference to parent death
- Reference to alcohol consumption

HERON EASED WHAT ey hoped was the final weed from its spot between the leaves of a rhubarb plant, careful to pull the entire root system free before tossing it into the wheelbarrow with the rest. Ey wiped the light sheen of sweat from eir face, then looked up to survey the garden for any remaining intruders. Only the neat rows of vegetables remained, soil dark and damp around them.

These days, with eir mother determined to make a living off selling her inventions, the garden was solely Heron's responsibility—which ey didn't mind. Ey liked the quiet, the steady rhythm, the progress as the plants grew and blossomed and bore fruit. Ey liked the smell of the dirt, the infinite variety in the plants, the insects that pollinated them...

If Tiel got his way, though, Heron was going to lose all of that. Living in town instead, hearing arguing people instead of the clucking of chickens, inhaling smoke instead of rain-soaked earth.

Sighing, ey unbent eir stiff knees and rose, rolling eir shoulders and stretching eir arms above eir head. With Ma away, off on her trip to the city fair that morning, Tiel had invited himself over tonight. Heron had reminded him, though, that that would mean waking up early tomorrow to make it back into town for work on time, and that had seemed sufficient to put him off the idea.

Guilt nagged em like a persistent fly, but ey just as persistently swatted it away. Ey was allowed to want some time to emself every so often. Ever since Ma had mentioned her trip, ey'd been looking forward to a quiet evening alone with a book. No clatter of tools from Ma's bedroom workshop, no trying to figure out if her mutterings were directed at em or just her talking to herself. Ey loved her, and they got along well for the most part—but it was still nice to have a break once in a while.

Of course, most people would relish the chance to have their lover over when they had the house to themselves... but then, most people weren't seeing Tiel. Maybe if he could sit still, could amuse himself while Heron read, or at least show an interest in what ey was reading, it would be different. Maybe if he could stop pestering Heron about moving to town with him for one moment...

Ey dropped eir arms with another sigh. At least ey'd succeeded in dissuading Tiel from coming by, and ey wouldn't have to face that tonight—

Something grabbed em around the ribs, and ey yelped, pulling away. When ey spun around, there was Tiel, sleeves rolled to the elbows, hands stained with ink, wearing the heeled boots that raised him two or three inches taller than Heron, elegant features crumpled into a laugh.

"For fucks' sake." Heron rolled eir eyes and gave Tiel a half-hearted shove, conveniently pushing him off the rhubarb plants he was trampling.

"Every time!" Tiel exclaimed through continued laughter. "I swear, you'll never learn." He grabbed Heron's hand, making a show of wincing at the dirt embedded in eir palm, and pulled em in for a kiss. "Impeccable timing on my part, don't you think? Looks like you've just finished for the day."

"Just about."

Heron turned to maneuver the wheelbarrow out of the garden and toward the compost heap. Tiel jogged to catch up, smacking eir ass as he fell into step beside em, making em jump, and Tiel laughed.

"Ah, I can't wait to have a night of peace and quiet," he remarked. "My parents are going to murder each other one of these days, I swear."

Here it came. Tiel would certainly use take this chance to segue into...

"Have you talked to your mum yet about leaving?"

The wheelbarrow hit a divot in the path, sending clumps of dirt bouncing into the air. Tiel fell back a step, giving Heron an extra moment to consider eir answer. "...No, not yet. She was so busy with fair preparations, you know, there really wasn't a good time."

"When *will* be a good time?" Tiel grabbed Heron's shoulder as he caught up again.

"Do I look like a fortune teller?" They'd reached the compost pile, and Heron shrugged Tiel's hand off and tipped the wheelbarrow forward, giving it a shake to get all the bits out.

"No, you look like a farmer's child who was meant for bigger things! Stop worrying about your mum and let yourself have this."

Heron rested the wheelbarrow on the ground again, and Tiel grabbed eir arms, spinning em to face him. Holding Heron in place, hands firm on eir biceps, he dropped his voice to an enticing whisper. "Come live with me, darling. Let me take you away from all this."

There was a time when Heron would have smiled at Tiel's theatrics. Ey had originally enjoyed that side of Tiel; it was what had drawn em in even before they'd met. The handsome man with the loud laugh and bold gestures, who veered into silliness at times, but whose confidence never wavered. When had that confidence become a wall holding Heron back, rather than a supportive foundation?

Heron closed the gap between them, pressing eir mouth to Tiel's, lifting a hand to run eir fingers down Tiel's chest.

"You're trying to distract me," Tiel murmured against eir lips.

"Is it working?"

Tiel pressed closer against em, sufficiently answering that question, and Heron let eir anticipated vision of the evening slip away. It was fine. Ey would have a night with Tiel, and ey would enjoy that instead.

In the dim light of morning, waking sore and cold and crammed against the wall—Tiel, still passed out beside em, had stolen all the blankets and most of the bed—Heron had to acknowledge that ey hadn't particularly enjoyed Tiel's visit. What was wrong with em? Ey hadn't been able to believe it when Tiel had approached em at last year's midsummer celebration, asking em to dance; ey'd thought it had been some joke, that Tiel and his friends were just waiting to laugh at em if ey agreed. The naive farm kid falling for the tricks of the sophisticated town lad. But it had been real—Tiel had made pleading eyes at em, and ey'd given in, and the grins Tiel had flashed as they danced had made eir heart flutter.

What had also been real, several dances and multiple drinks later, was Tiel pulling em aside, sliding a hand onto eir ass, and attempting to drunkenly kiss em. It had all become clear then—Tiel was just looking for a quick fuck. Heron had pushed him off and left, ignoring his confused "What? You don't want to kiss me?", berating emself for being so foolish as to think someone like Tiel could have an actual romantic interest in em.

The next day, though, the gifts had started. Baubles left with notes of apology, imploring forgiveness; cakes and sweets addressed to em, delivered in neat little boxes. Ma gave em significant looks and made comments about eir admirer, while Heron just felt humiliated. It was so *much*, so over-dramatic—it had to be Tiel's way of mocking em for not wanting to jump into bed with him. It was an expensive mockery—Tiel's family was decently well off, but not *wealthy*—but Heron couldn't imagine what other motivation Tiel could have.

Ey ignored it all, waiting for Tiel to get bored and give it up. But one day, as ey was leaving the barn, ey caught Tiel's red-faced form coming down the road from town, some kind of sapling balanced in his arms. Tiel's eyes had met eirs, and the look of mild panic on his face, the blush that had further reddened his cheeks, had seemed genuine. Something loosened in Heron's chest at the sight, and ey went to meet Tiel, taking the burden from his arms.

"You like plants," Tiel had blurted, anything but smooth. "So... this. It's an apple tree. I thought, something more practical..."

"What do you *want*?" Heron had asked, annoyed with emself for being slightly charmed by Tiel's flusteredness.

"I want you to know that I really am sorry for being

a drunken boor. Because... I like you. And I had hoped to spend more time with you."

Heron searched his face. Hair slightly mussed, dirt smudged on one cheek... If this was all a play to laugh at em, or just to get em in bed, Tiel was either an amazing actor, or somewhat insane. Somehow, him meaning it was the more logical explanation.

No one had ever gone to that much effort for Heron before. Much as ey'd hated to admit it, even to emself, it had made em feel a bit swoony. Somehow, Tiel liked em enough to pursue em; somehow, Tiel considered em worth getting to know.

Now, though, with Tiel having gotten what he wanted, Heron's heart and eir body and eir time, that all seemed to have worn away.

Tiel shifted beside em, arms reaching out to drag em closer, and whispered against eir neck, "Think of it. We could wake up like this every morning." That was supposed to sound nice; it was supposed to be what Heron wanted.

Instead, ey was glad when Tiel said he wouldn't be able to return that night. "Mum and Da said I'll have to work late to make up for starting late this morning," he said, rolling his eyes. The next day Heron's ma would be back, putting an end to the potential of privacy.

"Hey," Tiel said through a yawn as they stood together at the door. "Will you talk to your mum once she's back? For me?" He gave Heron the sad-eyed expression that had once made em feel something.

"All right," ey said, because what else could ey say? "I will."

Apparently ey was going to let emself be swept along with this plan of Tiel's. Ey knew ey didn't have to, knew ey had the power to dig in eir heels, but how was ey supposed to explain to Tiel beyond *That's not what I want*? Tiel wouldn't be satisfied with that answer, but when Heron tried to imagine what else ey might say, eir mind went fallow as a field in winter.

Was ey really still holding onto some ideal of "true love" that only existed in stories? Tiel's parents were constantly at each other's throats; Ma's partner had left her when Heron was young. Compared to those relationships, eirs and Tiel's was exemplary.

"Excellent!" Tiel leaned in to plant a kiss on Heron's lips before opening the door and stepping out backward. "Meet me for dinner at Keyn's afterward? I'll pay. We can make all our plans!" He waved as he turned around, leaving Heron staring after him. Apparently ey had just agreed to talk to Ma immediately upon her return—and start planning eir new life with Tiel immediately after that.

As it turned out, though, Heron wasn't able to ask Ma about Tiel's scheme the next day—because, by the time ey'd finished the chores, washed up, and dressed to leave for their dinner, she still wasn't back. If she'd set out in the morning, as she'd said she would, she should have arrived by now...

Ey tried not to worry. Maybe she'd had a late night with new friends, and had decided to leave later. Maybe she'd grown tired on the ride back and had decided to stop and rest. Maybe business had delayed her, her foot-pedal-powered laundry machine so popular at the fair that she'd been swamped with commissions. *You worry too much,* ey could hear her saying when ey asked where she'd been. *I'm supposed to be the parent here.*

At least it meant ey could postpone the big talk a bit longer. As a conciliation to Tiel, ey wore the red shirt he had given em, its ruffled sleeves always making em feel ridiculous even though Tiel said it looked dashing.

For as long as the farm was in sight ey cast glances over eir shoulder, watching for a glimpse of Old Pete pulling their wagon up the road from the opposite direction. But there was nothing.

"Look at you!" Tiel rose from the table where he waited in the midst of the inn's other guests, grabbing Heron's hands and looking em over. "All dressed up. Does this mean we're celebrating?"

Fuck, the shirt had been a mistake. "Not yet." Ey pulled eir hands free to take eir seat. "Ma isn't back yet."

"Really? Honestly, Heron, if I didn't know better, I'd say you're avoiding talking to her!"

"Are you accusing me of hiring thieves to waylay her or something?"

"No, not *that,* but *maybe* you saw her coming and ran away?"

Now of all times, Heron was not in the mood for Tiel's jokes. Ey just shook eir head and glanced around for the barkeep so ey could get a much-needed drink.

"Wait, are you actually worried?" Tiel stretched a hand across the table, and Heron gave in and slid eirs into it. "You know she probably just got wrapped up in something and ended up leaving late."

Heron couldn't argue with that after ey'd had the same thought emself, but those perfectly reasonable words weren't enough to quell eir buzzing nerves. Tiel didn't care about that, though; he only cared that Heron couldn't yet commit to his plan.

Why was ey having such uncharitable thoughts? Worry made em ill-tempered, apparently. If only ey had the spine to tell Tiel ey wasn't up to this dinner and wanted to go home. If only ey wasn't holding back in part because ey knew Tiel would argue.

They got food and drink; Heron picked at the former as Tiel prattled about getting em a job at his parents' office, how ey was certainly qualified since ey did all the bookkeeping for the farm, and then they'd work together and it would be so much more bearable with Heron there, they would never have to be apart and Heron would never know a moment's rest again...

No, wait, Heron's ill temper had supplied that last part. Eir gaze kept returning to the window as the day's light ebbed away. Ma might have gotten back by now, and would tease em about not being there to greet her. Tiel was right that she got distracted and absorbed in things easily—but that was the precise reason Heron worried about her. Ey could just see her setting out at sunset, not thinking about the impending darkness and how it would require her to spend a night in the forest.

"Heron?"

Fuck, ey hadn't been listening and now Tiel was going to give em shit for that. But no, actually, he was giving Heron a concerned look this time.

"Do you want to go back and see if your ma's home?"

Heron was nearly struck speechless at the suggestion. That Tiel would actually think of that, and offer it—it was nearly unprecedented. "Would you mind terribly?"

"I would mind only slightly," Tiel answered graciously. He stood, giving Heron no chance to argue. Heron downed the rest of eir drink and followed suit. But as ey turned away from the table, ey caught Tiel holding up a finger to someone at the bar—one of his friends, who gave him a nod in return. That explained it. Tiel was getting rid of em so he could spend time with someone more fun.

"You don't have to walk me out," Heron muttered as Tiel started to follow em to the door.

"Why, of course I do! What kind of man would I be if I left you to the mercies of the night fiends waiting to swoop down on unsuspecting travelers?" Apparently his high spirits were back now that he had the prospect of a pleasant evening before him again.

"You know there are—" ey started to return,

intending to remind Tiel that it really was dangerous to travel at night, and ey wasn't worrying over nothing. But Tiel went on over em.

"Or is it the Barringtons you're afraid of? Maybe they've just been waiting for an unsuspecting inventor to wander by in the dead of night, when their powers are at their height!"

This was why Heron had no patience for Tiel's dramatics anymore—he didn't know when they were appropriate and when they weren't. Tiel knew that Heron was not concerned about a family of mages who supposedly lived in a castle deep in the forest, where they conducted magical experiments. Ey'd loved those stories as a child—magic and castles and mysteries... But that was all they were. Stories.

"Be safe!" Tiel called as Heron walked away from the inn, his gallantry apparently extending only as far as the establishment's door. "Don't get eaten or magicked!"

Heron gave him a rude gesture without looking back, and Tiel laughed. He always laughed. He didn't fucking know when to stop laughing.

On the other hand... him not taking Heron seriously was the only reason Heron felt comfortable doing anything like pushing back.

HERON ARRIVED BACK to a still-empty house. Ey slept fitfully and woke feeling almost more irritated than worried. If Ma showed up today blithely declaring that she'd simply decided to spend an extra day in the city...

Ey was milking the goat when what ey assumed was a large insect buzzed in eir ear. Ey raised a hand to swat it away, and hit—metal? The thing fell to the barn floor with a soft thunk, and ey stared down at it. A golden cylinder lay in the straw, sporting two intricate metal wings, complete with individual feathers. As ey reached for it, it fluttered to life to hover in the air again.

At first ey drew back, staring at the thing with a frown, but then ey extended eir hand. The object—creature?—flew forward and alit on eir palm, wings going still.

Popping open the hinged cap on one end of the cylinder, ey found a rolled-up piece of paper inside.

Unfurling it revealed a note in Ma's handwriting.

Dearest Heron,

I hope I've not worried you! Just had a minor wagon accident, and managed to twist my ankle. You'll never guess where I'm laid up—the Barrington castle! I'm being taken good care of, and will be home in a few days, after I've rested up a bit more. Don't worry about me, just enjoy having more time with Tiel while I'm not around to get in the way!

Love,

Ma

Heron stared at the words even after ey'd finished reading. Eir first thought, ridiculous as it was, was that this was a scheme of Tiel's to tease em for eir fears. But… eir gaze shifted to the metal thing, which had apparently flown here on its own power. There was no way something like *this* was a joke. Which meant Tiel's quip about the Barringtons last night had actually been prescient. They were out there, and they had eir mother.

She might *say* she was fine, but why would some secretive mages who'd spent years lurking in the forest want to host an uninvited guest? It was more likely that she'd talked her way past their objections than that they had actually welcomed her. Or, that they had done the latter, but with nefarious intentions…

Ey glanced down at the golden contraption again. Of course Ma was predisposed to think well of them if they made things like this. She had very likely been too distracted by the charm of their inventions to notice any threat they posed.

Frustration sent em surging to eir feet. Tiel hadn't taken any of eir legitimate concerns seriously, and now Ma was being a fool and trusting some eccentric, powerful recluses with her life. Why was ey the only person who was fucking rational around here?

...Maybe rational was a stretch. Maybe it wasn't rational to finish the milking in a rush, herd the chickens back into the hen house, and toss some food and a spare set of clothes into a pack. Maybe it wasn't rational to stop at the neighboring farm, giving a hasty explanation and a promise to pay the family in exchange for tending to the animals if ey wasn't back by tomorrow morning, and then walk on until ey reached the edge of the forest.

But what else was ey supposed to do, wait around and simply hope Ma would turn up within the promised few days? Tiel would spin wild stories that wouldn't ease eir fears at all, and ey was bound to snap at some point, bound to say something ey'd regret. Besides, if Ma didn't come back within that time, ey was sure as fuck going to regret not going after her immediately.

Tiel would wonder where ey'd disappeared to, but it would take too much time to walk into town, and aside from that, ey wasn't about to subject emself to his arguments and declarations that ey was being ridiculous. Let him be the one worrying for a bit.

The shadowy trees beckoned, and Heron stepped forward into their embrace. Ey didn't know how far the castle was, or where it was, only that it was supposedly to the northwest, in the deepest part of the forest, somewhere off the road between here and the city. Ey didn't know how ey would find it, or if ey would at all. But fuck, ey was going to try.

The winged cylinder rested in eir pocket; it had stayed still since its arrival, wings wrapped around its body. But maybe...

Ey pulled it out, setting it on eir palm again. "Um. Hello?"

The thing startled em by whirring to life, rising into the air with a beat of its wings. "Fuck! Well. Okay. Can you... show me the way back to your home?"

It fluttered off ahead, then paused—waiting? Feeling almost dazed, half-convinced this was all a dream, Heron proceeded to follow.

Several hours later, Heron's winged guide turned off the main road and onto an overgrown track that wound its way deeper into the woods. Some of the stalks and saplings sprouting from it had been recently snapped, some of the flowers recently trampled. Heron paused to gulp some water, then continued down it.

Finally, when ey was starting to wonder whether it had been wise to trust the messenger creature, the trees thinned to reveal a wrought-iron gate set in a stone wall. Beyond it, atop a low hill, sat what could only be the fabled Barrington castle.

It was less the fortress Heron had always pictured and more a work of whimsy, bearing a single turret capped by a cone-shaped roof. The building's pale stone almost glistened, not looking at all weathered despite supposedly being decades old. Although the vines shrouding the turret and the rust coating the gate told a contrasting story of long disuse.

The gate was locked; eir metal guide had zipped through it and was now nowhere in sight. But—someone was coming down the path from the castle. Or no, not someone, some*thing*. Another metal creature, this one human-like, also gold, glinting in the sun as it walked on spindly jointed legs, somehow managing to move with grace. Its egg-shaped head was empty and smooth where a face should have been. It approached and, with the thin, bone-like fingers of one hand, fitted a key into the lock and pulled the gate open.

"Um. Thank you?" Heron went inside, even though that was exactly what all the stories said not to do in a situation like this. The creature—machine?—locked the gate behind em. Years ago, a traveling theater group had brought some things like it to town—automatons, able to move on their own through some mechanical process Heron didn't understand. They'd been jerky and awkward, though, and only capable of repeating a single, simple motion. Crude caricatures compared to this one.

The automaton began to climb the gradually sloping road, and Heron followed despite instinct telling em to bolt back the way ey'd come. It would have been better if the castle had appeared sinister; then ey would have *known* ey was in for something malicious, instead of being left merely suspicious and jumpy.

Beneath eir feet, the grass that had grown over the road had been recently flattened by something—Ma's wagon? To one side of the castle was an overgrown yard before a stone barn or stable, big enough to hold the wagon and Old Pete. On the other side, a low wall surrounded what had once been a garden. Now it was a wild tangle, shrubs stretching far out of their beds, paths overtaken by weeds.

The castle's heavy wooden door creaked as the automaton pushed it open and held it wide. All wisdom and sense told em not to set foot inside the building— that this was a trap, that the mages had used eir mother's note to lure em here. More people to experiment on, because apparently the stories were all true.

Well, if that were the case, Heron would walk to eir doom with eir head held high. For Ma's sake—and for the sake of discovering exactly what the fuck was going on here.

Stepping from the sunlight into the dim entry hall left em temporarily blind. When eir eyes adjusted, ey found emself standing on a marble floor, with an arched doorway across from em that looked to lead to a back corridor. It was flanked by two large marble staircases curving down from a landing overhead. The space was lit only by a row of windows near the ceiling, two stories above; the ones beside the door were covered by heavy curtains. Cold was already creeping in under eir clothes.

With an incline of its head, the automaton gestured em toward one of the staircases, and ey followed it up, because what else was ey to do?

Everything was spotless—no dust on the polished handrail, nor the old-fashioned landscape paintings that adorned the walls. The blue of the rug that stretched down the hallway was as vivid as if it had been dyed yesterday. It certainly felt like the home of mages—but where were they? A heavy silence pervaded the place; even the light scuff of eir footsteps seemed too loud.

Eir guide stopped before a door partway down the hall, gesturing to it with an elegant sweep of its fingers. Heron sucked in a breath and straightened eir shoulders. Ey was about to either shock eir ailing mother, or walk emself into a prison cell.

Ey opened the door. To a perfectly pleasant room, occupied by—Ma. She lay propped up on pillows in a canopied bed, wearing a wide, bemused smile, already reaching a hand toward em. "Heron! What are you doing here?"

Ey couldn't immediately come up with an adequate answer, but eir legs brought em to the bedside, where ey crouched and obligingly took her hand.

"I told you I'd be back in a few days!"

"You also told me you're staying with the *Barringtons*, for fuck's sake. I thought they weren't *real*. Of course I wasn't just going to sit around..."

She gave a slow, exaggerated head shake. "I knew you would worry. That was why I sent that note, to try to head it off..."

"That note was not the way to achieve that." Eir eyes found the injured ankle then, cushioned on a pillow, wrapped up in a bandage, with swelling visible at the edges. "Shit. Is it bad?"

"No, it's hardly anything. Just my body overreacting to a little sprain."

Ey squinted at her, and she stuck out her tongue. "I'm *fine*."

"If 'fine' means confined to a bed in some strangers' eerie magical castle, then yes, you are perfectly fine."

She just rolled her eyes, but with a smile.

"Really though, you have to tell me," Heron went on. "Is it actually a family of mages? And they were perfectly happy to take you in and nurse you back to health?"

This room's curtains were drawn wide, letting the sun illuminate a space comfortably appointed with a couch, tea table, desk, and washstand—a room meant for someone, someone who wasn't eir mother. Ey glanced back at the open door, as if one of them might be lurking there listening. All ey caught was a flash of the automaton's gold in the gloomy hall.

"Oh, no, no mages anymore. Didn't I say that in the note? I must have forgotten. No, there's just one man here now, all alone, poor thing. These metal servants aren't much company."

"Well, who the fuck is this man?"

Ma's eyes shifted beyond em, and Heron whipped back around. Now someone was standing in the doorway—a very human someone. Broad-shouldered, towering over a foot taller than the automaton behind him, with long, matted brown hair and an unkempt beard shrouding his face. A long, dark cloak covered the rest of him. As if he knew he were meant to be playing a role in a story, and had prepared for the part.

"Welcome," he said brusquely, voice low, slightly gravelly, as Heron scrambled to eir feet. His one visible eye was focused on em. "I'm sorry I wasn't more prepared for your arrival. It was... unexpected."

Heron frowned. "Well. I'm sorry I wasn't..." Ey'd meant to say something snarky in return, but eir wits had apparently deserted em. Ey shut eir mouth so ey wouldn't say, *That's what you get for practically kidnapping my mother.*

The stranger was silent, and Heron couldn't read his expression behind his curtain of hair. "Theo," Ma cut in. "Aren't you going to introduce yourself?"

Heron blinked. Ey should have expected her forwardness, and yet.

For one more long moment the man remained still. Finally he shoved half his hair back, revealing a pair of deep-set eyes in a pale face. "Theomer Barrington." He dipped a half-bow. "A pleasure to meet you." The words were a rote mumble.

"Heron Chaldriss. But I'm assuming you already

knew that." Ey gave Ma a sidelong glance, and she shrugged.

"You have... been mentioned, yes." The man crossed his arms, then dropped them back to his sides. If he was uncomfortable, Heron could understand why; ey would have been too if a pair of strangers had invaded eir home.

"What about offering em a bite to eat?" Heron's mother prompted. "Ey just walked all this way."

Theomer's gaze flicked to Heron. "Is that something you would like?"

"Um... yes, come to think of it." Ey lifted eir chin. "As long as it's not a bother."

Theomer gave a quick, curt nod. "Food," he ordered the waiting automaton before facing Heron again. "A meal will be brought shortly. I'll leave you and your mother to talk." He vanished through the door with a whirl of his cloak before Heron could muster up a "Thank you."

"All right, *please* tell me what's going on." Heron slumped into a chair, exhausted by eir bafflement as much as by the journey.

"Nothing's 'going on', Herry."

Ey cringed at the nickname. "You know what I mean. Why the fuck does he live here?"

"Well, I didn't ask him for his entire history."

"Gahhhh." Heron dropped eir head into eir hands. Maybe listening to Tiel yammer would have been preferable to this.

"Just relax! You're here now, even though you really shouldn't be, and you can see that I'm fine, so just enjoy the food—it's divine—and getting to sleep in a fancy bed tonight... Oh, but—the farm?"

"It's fine, the Stepfells are watching it. But look, tell me about your accident—what happened?"

She relayed the story, how she must not have supervised the re-loading of her machine carefully enough, the balance must have been off, so that when the wagon struck a stone, the rear axle snapped. She'd been flung from the seat and landed on her ankle. Fortunately she'd noticed the old road a short ways back, and managed to alternately hobble and crawl her way down it to the gate, where she'd yelled until one of the automatons let her in.

Of course. "So essentially, you didn't give him a choice but to help you."

"Better to ask forgiveness and all that." She grinned, shrugging one shoulder, but then her face drooped into seriousness. "Theo says he's already got the wagon fixed, I guess his little people went out and fetched it and replaced the axle. But, my machine..." She was looking down now, rubbing at a callous on her hand. "They can't fix that for me. It's bad; I'm going to need some new parts. Between that and my injury, it'll take me weeks to repair it..."

"Shit." Her wealthy client had given her permission to exhibit the machine at the city fair to drum up more customers before she delivered it to him. Delayed delivery would mean delayed payment.

"Not ideal, is it?" She glanced up at em with a forced smile. "But we'll be fine. We'll pull through."

Heron ran through figures in eir head, trying to determine if that was true. Ey'd been counting on that money now that they'd sold off their cow and one of the fields. They'd soon owe the neighbors for watching the farm, too...

"Don't you go worrying. I mean it. You've worried over me enough already, and I won't have any more. How's Tiel? Did you two enjoy your time together?"

"Oh, fuck. Tiel." At Ma's questioning look, ey went on, "I didn't tell him I was leaving. I should send him a note, see if I can borrow that messenger thing..."

The automaton's arrival with eir meal was a welcome interruption. Heron changed the subject to the fair, and Ma chattered about it while ey dined on roasted eggplant—which, ey had to admit, was indeed delicious.

Instead of writing to Tiel, Heron fell asleep after eating. Once ey'd finished, the automaton had shown em to the bedroom next door, where a folded cloak waited on the bed. Ey'd wrapped up in it immediately, both for the warmth and the comfort, then shuffled back to Ma's room with the overlong garment trailing on the floor behind em, letting her know through a yawn that ey was going to take a nap. Ey'd fallen onto the massive, soft bed, not bothering to pull shut the enclosing drapes—

what was ey, a princeling?—and drifted off.

When ey woke the room was dim, the sky faded to a pale gray-blue. Fuck, ey hadn't meant to sleep this long. Ey scrambled from the bed and into the hall, where the candles in the wall sconces burst to life as ey passed. Despite the practicality, ey almost found it irritating; it was as if the place were showing off.

Ey paused before Ma's door to give a quick knock, and after she called, "Come in!", ey entered. Inside Ma sat upright, fiddling with what looked like a detached automaton arm, a lamp burning bright on the bedside table. She spared em a glance before returning to it. "You're awake!"

"Ugh, just in time for it to get dark…"

"It's *fine*. No chores to get up for in the morning!"

"But we should get *going* first thing in the morning—you should be okay to travel by now, right? I can make you up a bed in the wagon, we could even leave the machine here for now if there isn't room and I could come back for it—"

"Is this about the money?" Her gaze lifted to fully meet Heron's then, her eyes bright. "Because you don't have to worry about that. While you were sleeping, we worked out a plan!"

"'We'?"

"Yes, me and Theo!"

Ey just stared at her. Ey was so tired of having to pry out answers that ey didn't have the will to even try this time. Apparently silence was as effective a prybar as any questions, though, for after a moment, she went on. "I'm going to stay here." Her eyes dropped; of course they did, because she fucking knew that was ridiculous and made no sense. "He offered me work," she continued, poking at the arm again. "See, a few of these metal people are broken, or damaged, and he's going to pay me to fix them, while I also get started repairing my machine."

Heron opened eir mouth to respond, but found ey didn't actually have anything to say. Everyone around em was busy chasing their whims, doing whatever the fuck they wanted and expecting Heron to just go along with it, no matter how it affected em.

How *this* particular scheme would affect em was that Tiel would probably take the opportunity to move into eir house, badgering em all the while about this being proof eir mother didn't want or need the farm, insisting that as soon as the season was over Heron put it up for sale and move into town.

"I'm going to go talk to him," was what finally came out. Ma looked up, face creased with surprise, but Heron shook eir head to ward off her questions. "I won't be long."

An automaton was lurking in the hall, because of course it was; the creepy fuckers were everywhere. Why did Theomer need the broken ones fixed when he already had so many? What did he need any of them *for*? Heron still didn't know what the fuck the man was even doing here, why he would choose to live in a castle deep in the forest, all alone.

"Where is he?" Heron demanded of the machine, and it clicked to life from its frozen posture, gesturing em to follow it down the hall, down the stairs, into the rear part of the main floor. To a small parlor, where it stood back to let em through the open door.

Two high-backed chairs sat before the crackling fire, a single lamp burning on the table beside one—beside Theomer, who sat with his hair pushed back behind his ears, a pair of spectacles resting on his nose, a book held up close to his face, catching the light.

"Oh." He started as Heron stepped into the room, dropping the book into his lap in a flutter of pages.

Heron winced. This wasn't quite what ey'd expected when ey'd gone to confront the man. "Sorry. Didn't mean to startle you."

"It's all right." Theomer pulled off his spectacles, folding them and setting them aside, shaking his head to let his hair fall in front of his face again. "Did you—need something?"

"I heard that my mum is going to be staying here?" Heron had remained in the doorway, and under Theomer's shrouded gaze ey crossed eir arms, lifting eir chin. Ey wasn't going to be intimidated.

"Sit." Theomer jerked a hand toward the other chair. Heron was about to tell him ey preferred to stand, not appreciating being ordered around, but then Theomer added, "Please," and Heron begrudgingly obeyed.

"I did indeed make your mother an offer of work,"

Theomer began. "Which she accepted. It wasn't meant to be done in secret, you just happened to be asleep…"

Heron squinted at him. "Yes, well, I was rather tired from walking all the way here."

"It's not a problem." Theomer shrugged slightly. "I'm glad to see you making use of your room."

Heron just snorted at that. Theomer sat forward, tilting his head so that his hair fell back a bit. "You don't trust me." Heron's instinct was to argue, as if it were an unfair accusation instead of the truth. Ey held eir tongue. "And I suppose that's fair. But my only goal here has been to help your mother. Have I done anything to make you think I have any ill intent?"

He had a point—enough of one to almost make Heron feel bad. Ma had practically trapped herself here; that wasn't Theomer's fault. And upon Heron's unannounced arrival, all he'd done was have his machines welcome em in and provide em with food, eir own room, and spare clothing.

"You… have not," Heron finally admitted, shifting in eir seat. "Well then. If you're not trying to make her stay, then…"

The idea that sprang into eir mind was ridiculous. And yet… "What if I were the one who stayed and worked for you instead?"

Whether from eir aversion to conceding defeat or eir dread of what would happen if ey returned home alone, or a combination of both, the words came out, and ey couldn't take them back. Ey wasn't sure ey wanted to.

The thought of getting away from Tiel, getting away from Ma for a bit even, being left in peace for once in eir life... It was so appealing it was suddenly all ey wanted. Theomer certainly didn't seem the type to bother em.

"You can repair magical machines?"

"You think my mum can? Okay, fine, she does have mechanical talent, and I don't have a speck of that, but I'm starting to suspect that you only offered her the work because she told you a sob story about us needing money. So let me stay and work on the garden instead. It's a mess, frankly, and that's an area I do have experience in."

A pause. Theomer was regarding em with his one visible eye, and Heron looked back, waiting.

"I don't have a particular use for the garden these days." Theomer's gaze moved to the fire. "I'd prefer the automatons getting mended."

Ey wanted to argue. Ey wanted to list out reasons why it made more sense to hire em than Ma, but they wouldn't be real reasons, would they? Eir proposal hadn't been rooted in logic.

That didn't mean ey wanted to let it go. It felt like ey had lost something, not just the minuscule battle with Theomer, but something more tangible, too. But— Theomer had decided. Ma would stay. Ey would go.

"All right. Fine. Just... don't let her do anything stupid," Heron muttered. "Make her stay in bed until her ankle's actually better."

"Are you leaving now?" Theomer sounded—

concerned? "You don't have to rush off, you're free to stay the night—"

"No, no, not *right* now. First thing in the morning, though, I'll be out of your way."

"It's no trouble, really." Theomer said it more to the floor than to Heron. It was time to put an end to this encounter, for both their sakes.

"Well." Ey rose and paced to the door, turning back as ey reached it. "Um, thank you for, you know…" Ey waved a hand, out of words and desperate to make eir escape.

Theomer nodded, murmuring, "Of course." Heron nodded back and then fled. Behind em, ey thought ey heard Theomer add, "Good night."

HERON SHUFFLED BACK into Ma's room and sank into the chair at her bedside under her bemused gaze. "Sorry," ey said through a long sigh, dropping eir face into eir hands. "I just—can't keep up with all this. I should have listened to your note, I should have trusted your judgment, instead of trying to play the hero and running all the way out here for no reason..."

The sheets rustled, and then Ma's hand was on eir knee, giving em a brief shake. "Hey, look though, now I've got you here to keep me company! I don't have to talk poor Theo's ear off anymore."

That gave Heron pause, and ey looked up. "Did he—spend time in here with you?"

"Yes, a bit." Ma sat back, brushing wisps of hair out of her face. "I'd pretend to get tired, though, to give him a break every so often."

"Well. That proves it, then. He's a perfectly decent

person and is certainly not going to imprison you here as his permanent inventor-servant."

Ey'd meant the statement to sound light, joking, but it came out slightly bitter.

"Herry." Ma's voice dropped into seriousness, and she watched em, eyebrows raised, until ey met her eyes. "What's wrong? Why are you so unhappy?"

Heron sighed, letting eir eyes close for a moment. "I'm... *embarrassed*. I was apparently wrong about everything, and to top it all off, I just made a fool of myself by asking him if *I* could stay instead of you."

Ma's face froze in an utterly baffled expression, and Heron felt a brief touch of amusement. Finally ey was the one causing someone else befuddlement. "I told him I could work on the garden. He just wants an excuse to give us money, he feels sorry for us I guess, because we're so poor while he lives here with magic and wealth to spare... So it's just as well me as you, right? But it doesn't matter, because he said no. I guess he likes you better."

"But why would you even want to stay here? Don't you want to get back to Tiel?"

"No, frankly, I... kind of wanted some time away from him." Ey mumbled the words, glancing away again. Ey didn't normally talk to Ma about these things, but here in this strange place with nothing else to occupy either of them, there was no way to avoid being at least a little bit honest.

"Oh." Heron could practically hear gears turning in her head; she must've been piecing things together, offhand remarks of eirs, observations of eir interactions with Tiel... If only Tiel himself would do the same.

"I could talk to Theo." Ma regarded em, chin propped on her hand. "Tell him I changed my mind?"

"No, please don't. He'd know I said something to you, it would be even more awkward... Besides, it makes more sense for you to stay anyway. You'll get to work on these mechanical wonders..." Ey swallowed back eir frustration and put on a teasing tone. "Maybe I should say goodbye for good. Not sure you'll *want* to come back to the farm after this."

"Oh, of course I will. If only to fetch my lucky screwdriver." She smiled at em, and ey rolled eir eyes good-naturedly. Ey thought they were done then, enough serious conversation for one night, but then she went on, "Really, though, about Tiel..."

"It's fine. It's just me being stupid."

"You know that if you're not happy, you don't have to stay with him."

Heron did know that, abstractly. But practically, ey hadn't ever really considered it an option. It had taken em so long to come to eir decision, all through Tiel's extended courtship, and in the end, ey'd made eir choice. It wasn't a marriage pact, a pledge to be Tiel's partner for life, but it had meant something to em; ey wouldn't have committed to Tiel if ey hadn't been serious about it. And ey had been, because Tiel had proved he had real feelings for Heron. Heron had thought that was enough.

How did one explain they weren't happy? How did one admit they'd changed their mind? How did one face the hurt in their lover's eyes? How could one bear seeing their former lover on the street?

What if one regretted their choice, only realizing how fortunate they had been after it was too late?

"I know," ey told Ma. "I just... don't know if I'm ready for that yet. Although..." A long sigh escaped. "He wants me to move to town with him." There it was, the words finally spoken. Ironically, Tiel would not be happy about it if he knew the context.

"And you're not ready for that, either."

"I never *will* be ready for it. I don't want to live there, I don't—want to live with him."

"You know you can tell him that."

"I can *try*, but he won't understand. It'll all be a huge mess, and..." Ey didn't know where that "and" led, but dread roiled in eir stomach at the thought of it. "Look, can we not talk about this anymore? I need to just... not think about him for a bit longer."

"All right... Just—one more thing? Don't be so hard on yourself about all this. You're wound tighter than a clock spring, holding onto all these fears and doubts... You should try to let go, and trust your heart."

"If my heart's saying anything right now, it's that I shouldn't abandon you in a forsaken castle."

"Oh, stop trying to distract me. Besides, didn't we already establish that I'm wiser than you give me credit for? Maybe you should consider heeding my advice."

Ey sighed dramatically. "I'll... consider considering it."

She snorted. "I suppose I'll take that."

Ey ducked out to visit the washroom, and then sought out an automaton, finding one standing against the wall at the top of the stairs. "Can you show me to the library?" ey asked. Ey was all talked out, but ey needed some way to occupy emself and Ma. At home ey often read aloud to her in the evenings while she worked; she may not have always paid attention, but ey still enjoyed it. And ey was itching to see what books a mages' library held.

The automaton's only answer, though, was to cock its head briefly before returning to its previous rigid posture. "No?" Heron asked. "What, you don't have a library?"

It repeated the gesture. No library didn't seem right, but then, nothing about this place did. Maybe the mages had taken all the books with them when they'd left.

Ey could find Theomer and ask him about it—the library, the mages, everything. But ey wasn't about to make a dunce of emself in front of the man again. Ma would learn the story, or at least bits of it, and write em long gossipy letters when she did. For tonight... well, ey might as well return to the blissful oblivion of sleep.

Upon waking up in the morning, Heron immediately

wished ey hadn't. The luxurious bed tempted em to roll over and close eir eyes again, forget about eir responsibilities... But no. No, it was time to be a fucking grownup and go home, pay the Stepfells for their work, tackle the day's remaining tasks, and—face Tiel. Apologize for vanishing, especially since ey had forgotten to write, and then... well, whatever came after that.

Ey sighed and slipped from the bed, not bothering to pull on eir clothes yet; ey hadn't brought a nightshirt, and had been sleeping in only eir drawers. Padding to the door barefoot to head to the washroom, ey pulled it wide and stepped into the hall—and nearly ran into Theomer.

"Shit—" Ey drew back quickly, and Theomer did the same, leaving a large gap between them.

"Heron. Sorry." Had the man been hurrying? He spoke quickly, his breathing audible, and actually shoved his hair out of his face to meet Heron's eyes. "Your mother's gone."

Heron blinked, speechless. Horrified, barely comprehending—

Theomer's eyes widened. "No, sorry, not like that. She's fine, I mean, I assume she is. But she left. Took your horse and the wagon."

"The fuck." Heron slouched against the door frame, trying to process both eir relief that eir mother hadn't fucking died in the night, and also that she had—left? Abandoned em here, sneaking off without a word to either em or Theomer.

"She... left a note." Theomer lifted his hand jerkily, offering Heron a sheet of paper, and ey stepped forward to take it.

Dearest Heron & Theo,

Please forgive me! After talking with Heron yesterday, I realized this is for the best. Theo, ey will do wonders for your garden if you just give em a chance. I really don't think I have the skills to fix your machines, anyway. I'm just a humble, non-magical tinkerer! Besides, I really need my own workshop and tools if I'm going to repair my machine properly. Don't be angry, please? Heron, I'll see that the farm is taken care of. Don't worry!!

Write me with one of those delightful letter-delivery machines so I know you don't hate me, won't you? Even if it is to scold me.

Love and kisses,

Ma

With a disbelieving huff, Heron looked back up at Theomer.

"Does she... often do things like this?" Theomer asked.

"Trick someone into hiring her child as a gardener? No, this would be the first time." Ey sighed. "But, I can't say I'm exactly surprised..."

Theomer folded his arms, cloak settling around them. "The... conversation between the two of you that she referenced...?"

"Fucking..." Heron let out a long sigh. "I just told her that I asked you if I could stay in her place, and that you turned me down."

Theomer's eyebrows rose slightly, and Heron rolled eir eyes. "All right, fine, I said that I would've liked some time away from... things. But I told her it was fine, I did not ask her to do... this."

"Oh, I believe you." Theomer raked his hair back again, eyes drifting away into the distance. "Well. Now you're here, and she isn't."

"I don't have to stay, though, I can walk back, I did it once already—"

"But you need money."

"We'll be fine, we'll work it out."

"Let me speak plainly." Now Theomer's gaze settled on Heron again, and ey raised eir chin in response. "You can stay. Have your time away, fix up my garden. I don't *need* it, but it would be nice to have it not be... that. Anymore."

Heron squinted at him. "We don't need charity."

"And like I said, I don't need my garden tended." Theomer shrugged. "It's your choice."

Here ey was again, victim to other people's schemes and whims, going along because it was easier than resisting. Except... this one *had* started out as eir idea. Ey was certainly going to have words for Ma about making it happen in this underhanded manner, but... ey had wanted this. Why not let emself have it?

"...All right. Fine. I'll be your gardener. Might as

well, since I'm here."

Theomer looked startled, but he quickly composed himself and nodded. "Very well. Whenever you're ready, I'll show you to it."

Only then did Heron remember eir state of undress. Hastily crossing eir arms over eir chest, ey answered, "All right great, I'll find you. When I'm ready." Ey turned away, hopefully before Theomer could notice eir reddening face.

Properly dressed and stomach full, Heron found Theomer in the parlor. A set of sheer curtains covered the windows, keeping the space dim. Theomer held an open book, but he didn't have his spectacles on. "All right," he declared, rising when Heron had barely entered the room, and Heron backed up again to let him lead the way, cloak billowing dramatically behind him. Down the hall, through a kitchen, then out a side door into the erstwhile garden.

"All right," Theomer repeated, stopping at the edge of the tangle to point to a shed nearly hidden behind the trailing branches of a weeping willow. "Tools are in there, and I'll send out some of the servants to help you. They should be able to handle basic tasks."

Heron stared at the mess before em. Ey had experience with plants, yes, but ey'd never dealt with anything like this. "Is there... anywhere in particular you want me to start? Or, anything particular you want...

done with it?"

"I trust your judgment," Theomer answered simply. "I'm looking forward to seeing something new. But, you should know that you're going to encounter some things that are... unusual." Heron glanced at him sidelong, but Theomer wasn't looking at em, instead gazing out over the garden. "Unnatural, I suppose is a better word. Nothing dangerous, just some magical tampering here and there."

Heron narrowed eir eyes. "What kind of tampering?"

"Mmm..." Theomer glanced around, fixing after a moment on the corner opposite the shed. He strode over to kneel in the thicket of leaves at the edge of the path. Heron followed as he parted the branches of some shrubs, revealing a glimpse of purple. Eir eyebrows lifted as more came into view—a crocus, which for one thing shouldn't have been blooming this time of year, but more remarkable was its size. Five times larger than an ordinary crocus, if not more.

"...Oh. Unnatural. I see."

"There are some even stranger ones, somewhere in that mess." Theomer stood, glancing over his shoulder. Heron decided not to press for more details. Ey would discover them emself soon enough.

"Well then." Theomer shook out his cloak and brushed a leaf from his hair. "Is there anything else you think you'll need?"

"Um, no, not now. Thank you."

Theomer gave a rather stiff nod. "All right." Then he was retreating toward the castle, leaving Heron alone with the jumble of mystery plants waiting to be tamed—or waiting to try to eat em. Ey gave the mess a dubious squint before pushing the willow branches aside to explore the shed.

Eir first task, ey quickly decided, would be to pull the weeds that had grown up in front of the shed door, nearly blocking it from opening. Four automatons had trooped out in Theomer's wake, and at Heron's behest they got to work, wielding shears and hoes with ease as they slowly cleared their way down two of the paths further into the garden. Once those were minimally passable, ey would be able to get a better idea of what ey'd be working with.

With the shed door cleared, ey stood and stretched and wandered down one of the paths to check their work. All fine, just what Heron had wanted from a preliminary pass—except for a lone forsythia shrub whose branches still extended across the path. "Missed one!" ey called, then stood and waited while a shears-bearing automaton marched back to em.

Instead of lifting the blades to the plant itself, though, it offered them to Heron. "Well. If you insist..." With a satisfying *snick*, ey clipped off a few branches. As ey opened the shears to cut the next bunch, though, new growth sprang from the chopped ends, stretching out before em, buds forming and bursting into flowers and leaves before eir eyes, until it was as if ey hadn't trimmed it at all.

Ey glanced down to where the fallen pieces still lay—along with some additional ones, more than ey had cut. With an apologetic grimace, ey returned the shears to eir companion. "I see. Guess we'll have to reroute the path in this spot or something." The automaton inclined its head, then strode off to continue its labor.

Hours later, with the sun high overhead and sweat sheening eir skin, ey ducked into the kitchen for a meal. A pitcher of water, a cup, and a washbasin awaited em on the table—as did an oversized book, its title engraved in gold lettering: *Chespin's Illustrated Guide to Cultivars*. Heron cracked it open to find it full of marvelously detailed drawings and descriptions of plants of all kinds. Ey got lost in it for a bit, forgetting to request food until an automaton came to stand pointedly at eir side. "Where did this come from?" ey asked, because apparently there were books here somewhere after all—which should have occurred to em sooner, since ey'd seen Theomer reading one yesterday.

Of course the machine didn't answer. Had one of them brought it here? Or had Theomer delivered it himself, slipping back into the kitchen while Heron worked, pausing, perhaps, to stand at the window and see how it was going?

...Most likely not. Watching someone pull weeds was the most boring thing possible, at least according to Tiel. Heron had countered the claim with, "You could help," but Tiel had made a fuss about his clothes getting dirty.

Ey ate a salad that the automaton produced from the larder, the vegetables as crisp as if they'd just been sliced, and then returned to work. The afternoon was productive and uneventful, save for a startling moment when a cluster of morning glories clinging to a rotting trellis turned toward em in perfect synchronization as ey approached. "Yes, I know I'm chopping up some of your friends, but you don't need to be creepy about it," ey muttered once ey'd recovered eir breath.

There was also one point when ey heard music, muffled but distinct, coming from the direction of the castle. Apparently Theomer played... something. Heron couldn't tell what instrument it was, but the tune was a bit melancholy, slow and almost foreboding. Incongruous with the bright day, with the riot of plant life around em.

Finally, ey took eir growing hunger as a signal to be done for the day and headed inside, leaving the automatons to put away the tools. Ey arrived at the washroom intending to clean up before eating, but instead of just the pitcher and washbasin, a warm bath awaited em, the tub that had previously occupied one corner now standing in the middle of the floor, full of steaming water. Ey stared at it, at the towel and bar of soap resting on the low table beside it. Was ey an employee, or an honored guest?

Metal footsteps sounded behind em, and an

automaton strolled in with a tray of food. Had Theomer planned all this?

It was a bit odd, and certainly unexpected, ey wasn't about to turn it down. Ey ate while soaking eir aches away, marveling at the luxury. Did Theomer eat dinner like this every night? Probably not, judging by the state of his hair...

Maybe it was time ey sought answers to some of eir questions about the man, and about this place. Ey wasn't about to ask Theomer outright; it would be rude, and ey wasn't at all sure Theomer would actually answer. But it couldn't hurt to do a little investigating. Just so ey could stop wondering all the time, and perhaps have some stories to entertain Tiel with, so that he'd be less annoyed at eir vanishing. Ugh, ey still hadn't written yet...

With eir hunger satisfied and eir body thoroughly steeped in warm water, the soft bed waiting down the hall called to em. Investigating would happen, as would letter-writing. Tomorrow.

MIDWAY THROUGH THE NEXT MORNING, as Heron freed an ornamental maple tree from the grip of a dead vine, the buzz of mechanical wings announced the approach of a messenger gadget. This one held two sheets of paper, the first of which read:

Dearest Heron,

I'm writing to let you know I'm back home safe and sound—yes, I did ~~steal~~ borrow one of these, but I'm sure Theo won't mind! I was hoping I would have heard from you by now; I know you would never snub your old mother, so I can only assume you're busy with your new duties. But please, drop me a line when you can? I want to hear how things are going!

I've seen the doctor in town; she says my ankle will be fine, I just need to keep resting it. Fortunately I can work while I do so. It's a bit lonely here without you, but Theo already sent quite a generous sum of money, so I've been able to hire Iggy to take care of the farm work while you're gone.

Are you and Theo getting on? I hope he isn't upset with me. Oh, but please tell me he's done something about that hair!

I saw Tiel and explained the situation to him—about your working there, I mean, nothing else. He gave me a letter to include. Don't worry, I didn't read it!

Write me soon? I hope you can see that I did this as a kindness. I want you to have the time away that you need, and really, I'm much more comfortable at home (even if I would have loved to get to play with those machines some more).

All my love,
Ma

Ey shook eir head; she couldn't even give em a day before hassling em to write. Of course, ey owed Tiel a letter anyway...

Ey almost wanted to set his note aside without reading it, put it off until later, but ey made emself slide Ma's behind it.

My dear Heron:

I never thought I'd be writing to you like a lovesick maiden in a story, but since you've apparently been entrapped in a magical castle like a lost adventurer, I suppose it's appropriate. Your mum told me you ran off after her and now you've gotten yourself stuck there?? Or, sorry, you're <u>working</u> there, but I can't say I really understand why...

Anyway, you confuse me, you baffle me, you leave me puzzled and mystified, but I miss you and hope you're all right? Your mum assures me you are, but to be honest I'd rather hear it from you. Out there all alone with some mysterious sorcerer... If I don't hear from you soon, I'm going to have to come after you myself to enact a dramatic rescue. I would hate to find you've been turned into a frog, or perhaps a literal heron—that one might actually be funny, come to think of it...

I remain forever yours, waiting ardently for your reply,
Tiel

Heron's shoulders slumped with exasperation. Everything was a game with Tiel; everything was a joke. He wasn't even properly upset at Heron's lack of communication.

That evening, ey forewent a bath and wrote back to both of them.

Dear Ma,

Why yes, I have indeed been busy with the job that you so underhandedly foisted upon me. I'm not angry with you, just... mildly vexed, perhaps. The man already told me no; you put us both in quite an awkward position. But I suppose it worked out, because he is all right with my staying on. And gods, the garden needs the help. It's got magical plants, did you know? It feels like they're watching me while I work.

I haven't seen Theomer himself much. Seems very quiet, reserved. Letting me do whatever I want with the garden. And no, no changes to his hair. What, did you think he was going to clean up for me, his temporary gardener?

I'm glad you're safely home, and have seen a doctor, and

that the farm's being cared for. I'm still... let's say, uneasy about all this, but so far I guess I have no complaints.

I'll write again soon.

Love,

Heron

P. S. I'm enclosing a letter to Tiel—don't read it!

Dearest Tiel,

Guess what, I <u>have</u> been transformed into an actual heron, but a very clever one that can hold a pen in its beak, so it won't impede our correspondence. Can't do much in the way of gardening, but I can fly around and flap my wings and scream at the metal people who staff this place, so at least the work is still getting done.

I'm sorry I didn't let you know before I went off after Ma. Her letter was maddeningly vague and caught me off guard, and I let my fears run away with me. Or I ran away with them? Anyway, maybe Ma didn't tell you, but it's all due to her machinations that I'm here. Theomer, who is not a mage, is paying me handsomely for taming his mess of a garden, and since we're a bit hard up at the moment due to Ma's accident, I've got to stay on for now. But I'll come back soon, at least for a visit. Don't miss me too much.

Yours,

Heron

Finally, at the end of Heron's third day of work—another day where ey hadn't caught even a glimpse of

Theomer, although ey had heard the music again—ey decided to start eir investigation.

Eir own room revealed little; it had clearly belonged to someone once, with small tells like an ink stain atop the vine-carved desk and a slight path worn in the thick, soft rug between the bed and the wardrobe. Wardrobe and desk were empty of personal effects, though, and there was nothing else to give away who they had belonged to. Nor what had become of that person.

Down the hall were several closed doors, presumably more bedrooms, and ey didn't disturb those. Ey'd already seen Ma's, which hadn't held anything of interest, and one of the remaining ones had to be Theomer's. Ey wasn't about to investigate *that* thoroughly.

Ey'd seen most of the first floor already: parlor, kitchen, a glimpse at the adjacent dining room. Picturing the layout in eir mind told em there had to be at least one more room ey hadn't seen yet, but if Theomer was in the parlor now, he'd hear Heron blundering about. Which left the third floor.

The stairway waited at the end of the hall, dark, polished wood gleaming. If Theomer happened to be up there, ey would just say ey was looking for... the library, yes. Ey could tell him ey'd already tried asking the automatons.

The top of the stairs revealed not a library, but a single large, open space encompassing the entirety of the third story. Large windows let the light of the lowering sun pour in, and a large swathe of empty stone floor, etched with faded symbols, took up the middle of the room. A row of workbenches stood against one wall, scattered with an assortment of golden parts, tools hanging in a row above them. In the far corner was another door—that would lead to the turret. Did ey dare venture up there?

Not yet. Ey approached the workbenches; apparently whatever kept the rest of the place clean didn't apply up here, for dust coated the surfaces and the pieces of one or more disassembled automatons that lay atop them. How long had this space sat like this, unused? Why had it been abandoned in the first place?

A cough came from behind em, and ey jumped and spun around. Theomer stood at the top of the stairs, regarding em with a squint from behind his hair, a hand up as if to shield his eyes from the light.

"...Hi." Heron refused to apologize. Ey hadn't been forbidden to explore.

"Good evening. Did you—want a tour of the place?"

It was a tentative offer, not a scolding, but Heron still felt the humiliation of being caught. Eir library excuse suddenly seemed transparently false. "No, I... think I've seen enough. Um, nice workshop."

Theomer glanced around, as if he'd forgotten what the room was, then nodded. "Mm."

"So, uh..." Heron went on, not sure what Theomer wanted if he wasn't going to tell em to get out. "This was where the mages did their... mage things?"

"Indeed. Mage things."

Theomer remained straight-faced, voice even, but Heron still wondered if he was mocking em. Ey huffed. "Well, *I* don't know what weird experiments they were up to. Except creating metal creatures and creepy plants." Ey strode across the room to the stairs—to Theomer, who stood blocking eir way down. "Well," ey said as ey stopped. "I'll be off to bed now; another long day of work tomorrow..."

"It's going well?" Theomer rocked back on his heels, giving Heron more space. "Is there anything you need?"

"It's fine, yeah. I'm all set for now. Still got a lot of basic clearing and trimming and such to do."

"You know you don't have to spend the entire day working."

Heron shrugged. "Not really sure what I'd do with myself if I didn't."

"Actually I was... going to ask... Would you like to join me for dinner tomorrow?"

The words caught Heron off guard. Ey studied Theomer's face; it revealed no falseness, no games. His gray-blue eyes looked back at em; he'd pushed his hair out of the way at some point. His lips were parted questioningly. Right—he was waiting for an answer.

"Um. Yes, all right. Sure," ey found emself saying, because ey had no reason to refuse. "One of the automatons can fetch me when you're ready?"

"Yes. Good. And," Theomer added as he turned, descending one stair before looking back at Heron, "you're free to look around more if you like. Just— avoid the turret, it isn't safe these days."

"All right," Heron replied as Theomer departed, the steps creaking under his feet. Odd that the turret would have fallen into a dangerous state when the rest of the castle seemed in perfect condition, and it made em want to at least peek inside, but ey felt compelled to respect the man's wishes after being caught snooping around his home.

Ey lingered at the top of the stairs until Theomer had disappeared from sight. Then, after one more glance around the room, revealing no further insights, ey descended as well.

In the garden the next afternoon, Heron uncovered a non-magical surprise. Beneath a thick layer of ivy, which ey had to wrestle free from its hold on the far wall, was a fountain, its series of cascading stone basins filled with plant detritus instead of water. A sculpture atop it depicted two figures dancing, one pair of hands clasped while they held each other with the other. The taller one had rugged features; the shorter one was missing its head.

With the clinging vines and layers of dead leaves cleared away, ey caught flashes of color amidst the remaining grime in the base. Rubbing a spot clear with eir thumb revealed a lovely, soft blue tile. Ey had one of the automatons fetch em a wet cloth and used it to scrub away the dirt until all of it was clean and shining. Never mind that other tasks were perhaps more pressing.

When ey got to eir feet, knees aching, ey found an automaton waiting behind em. "Fuck, dinner..." Ey'd gotten so absorbed ey'd forgotten about it, which had been nice, because ey was inexplicably nervous. What would ey and Theomer have to talk about? Would the whole thing be stiff and formal and awkward?

Ey darted inside to scrub up and put on eir single clean shirt; ey'd washed eir worn set of clothes emself the other day, not about to ask anyone, even the automatons, to do that for em. Once in a semi-presentable state, ey strode into the dining room.

Theomer awaited em, sitting at the end of the row of three chairs that lined one side of the table, which bore a red brocade cloth. Places had been set before him and the seat opposite. His hair was drawn into a tail now, and Heron couldn't be certain, but it looked like an attempt at combing it had been made. His eyes met Heron's as ey approached. "Good evening."

"Good evening." Heron drew out the heavy wood chair and sank onto its cushioned seat, keeping eir back straight. "Sorry if I kept you waiting."

"Not at all."

Heron touched one of the two silver forks beside the plate, and when ey accidentally pushed it out of its rigid alignment, tried to adjust it back. Fortunately, before ey could do or say anything else foolish, an automaton emerged from the kitchen bearing a tray laden with two bowls.

"Smells good," Heron remarked.

"Indeed."

The automaton set a bowl before Heron first, and ey sat gazing down at the soup, a thick broth with potato chunks floating in it, breathing in its delicious, oniony steam while Theomer was served. As the servant withdrew, Theomer pointedly lifted his spoon, and Heron shook emself and did the same.

For a bit, only the clinking of silver on porcelain broke the silence as Heron tried to think of something not-inane to say. The soup tasted as good as it smelled, at least, but that was not an adequate conversation topic...

Finally, ey started with, "Thank—", meaning to express eir gratitude for the plant book, which had provided useful pruning guidance for certain plants and confirmed eir suspicions that some should not have currently been growing. But Theomer started speaking at the same time, and then they both stopped. Heron clamped eir mouth shut before opening it again to blurt, "You go."

Theomer cleared his throat. "I was just going to ask if you've had word from your mother?"

"Oh, yes, she made it back in one piece; she sent a message using one of your little gadgets she stole."

"Hardly stealing when she sent it straight back," Theomer returned mildly.

"Except I already wrote back to her, to assure her

neither of us hates her, so you might have to consider it stolen after all…"

Theomer lifted one shoulder. "I don't mind. I'm glad someone can make use of them."

"So, um, from what I saw yesterday…" Heron began, treading carefully but unable to resist asking, "I'm assuming the mages invented all these… contraptions themselves?"

"Indeed," Theomer answered as one of said contraptions cleared their empty bowls away and another emerged with the next course, pies wafting the scent of spiced meat.

"They've been very helpful in the garden," Heron went on when Theomer didn't seem inclined to continue. "I could use some on the farm. It's probably a good thing Ma didn't get to dive into tinkering with them, she very likely would have tried to kidnap a few."

"I can imagine her ordering a team of them around." Theomer smiled then, closed-mouth but full, and Heron had to stop emself from staring. It transformed his face, making him look younger. Less careworn.

Refocusing on the conversation, Heron smirked back and shook eir head. "She would name them all too, paint faces or markings on them to tell them apart and call them Rupert and Tiffany or something…"

"I never thought of that. Might be nice to give them some personality."

"Hmm, we could call that one 'face-dent', and that one 'creaky leg'…"

"Ah, if only she had repaired them, they wouldn't earn such ignoble titles."

"Unfortunately it's probably only going to get worse with the garden work. Soon we'll have 'missing finger' and 'dirt-in-joints'."

Theomer chuckled softly, then ducked his head, focusing on cutting his pie. Heron felt inordinately pleased at successfully joking with him—something ey wouldn't have predicted even yesterday. This whole dinner situation was going better than ey'd expected.

"I've found some of those magical plants you talked about," ey said as ey sliced into eir own pie. "They were a bit unnerving at first, but I'm getting used to them."

"Mmm," Theomer answered through a mouthful.

"Oh, and today I found the fountain," Heron added. "Too bad about the statue, but looks like it's been broken for a while? That tile is in perfect condition, though. I'd love to paint our barn that color..."

Theomer set down his fork and glanced up at em, eyes bright. "Ah, the fountain. I'd nearly forgotten. It was my favorite spot as a child. I liked to sit on the edge with my feet in the water on hot days, daydreaming up stories about the two lovers. In the statue, I mean; it wasn't broken then. The sky always looked blue behind them in the reflection, even on cloudy days."

That had to be the most Heron had heard Theomer speak at once—and it was an anecdote about his past, even. It felt like he had entrusted Heron with a gift.

Ey could have said, *So, you grew up here?*, but ey

didn't want to press. Better to let Theomer share things in his own time. "That sounds nice," ey answered, sincerely. "I did that too as a kid—making up stories, I mean. Now I mostly just read ones by other people. Um, what were you reading the other day, if I can ask?"

"Oh, it was one of the epics—*Peril to the Foes of Avra.*"

"Ah, that's one of Ma's favorites. I've read it to her countless times while she worked."

"Have you?" Did Theomer's voice hold a note of wistfulness? "She seems kind. A bit overwhelming, perhaps, but kind."

Heron snorted. "You can say that again. I love her, and I know I'm lucky to have her, but sometimes that house does not feel big enough for the two of us."

"She told me about your farm. What animals do you have?"

Heron told him, about the animals and more, and Theomer seemed to listen to every word, asking questions, clearly engaged. That shouldn't have been surprising. Why was it surprising? All this time shut up here alone, it made sense that Theomer was interested in hearing about the outside world. Even something as mundane as farm life.

Dessert was plates of syruped pear, which apparently Heron ate with such gusto that Theomer asked if ey'd like a second helping. "Oh, no, I couldn't, I'm too full. Thank you, though." Eir gratitude extended beyond the offer of additional fruit, but ey wasn't quite sure how to convey that.

Theomer nodded. "Of course." He drew in a breath; swallowed. "Tomorrow—would you like…"

Was he… nervous? "Dinner again?" Heron asked, to save him. "Yes. I'd like that."

The corners of Theomer's mouth twitched upward ever so slightly. "All right. Good."

"I… wanted to ask," Theomer said, midway through dinner the next day. His eyes were on his plate, his fork twirling a flaky piece of salmon. "You mentioned reading aloud to your mother. Do you enjoy it?"

Heron had not expected that question. Ey took a moment to find eir answer. "I do, yeah. I like the performance of it, I guess, making the words exist outside my head."

"Well, in that case, I wondered if… perhaps… you'd read to me sometime? I find reading a bit strenuous— weak eyes." He finally glanced up at Heron then, the eyes in question peering from under his dark brows. "I'd pay you extra for it."

"Oh." Heron hadn't been prepared for that, either. "No, you don't have to pay me. I'd be happy to do it."

"You're sure? I don't want to intrude."

Heron shook eir head. "No intrusion at all. I could start tonight, even."

Now Theomer lifted his chin, fully meeting Heron's gaze. "All right. If you'd like."

Was that... *anticipation* ey felt? It had been, what, four days since Ma had left, and already ey was desperate for human company? No wonder Theomer had made the suggestion, when he'd been here alone for who knew how long...

Well, it was nice that they were getting along. Nice that they could provide company to each other.

Once the meal was over they relocated to the parlor, lamps flickering to life upon their entry. They each took one of the fireside chairs, and Heron lifted Theomer's copy of *Avra* from the side table, opened it to his marker, and started reading.

Ey felt a bit dry-mouthed and unpracticed at first, self-conscious under Theomer's gaze. Ma never watched em while ey read, always fiddling with something, muttering to herself under her breath, not paying any attention half the time.

When ey'd asked Tiel, early on, if he liked to read at all, his answer had been, "I stare at books all day, I'm not about to devote my free time to them too." Perhaps he would have been amenable to being read to, but Heron had been too shy to suggest it then, suspecting that Tiel would just be bored and distracted, or would find something about eir performance to laugh at.

Despite the unaccustomed audience, before long the familiar words swept Heron away, and ey fell into the rhythm just like all the times ey'd read to Ma. Ey let the cadence guide eir voice, going hushed at the solemn moments, louder and grander at the dramatic ones.

When ey reached the end of Part III, ey lifted eir head, almost dazed, returning to the room. And to Theomer, who still watched em steadily.

"Um. Well, I suppose I should stop there for the night." Ey smiled sheepishly as ey closed the book.

"Thank you," Theomer said, softly. Heron acknowledged it with a quick, jerky nod.

The moment stretched, lingered, as neither of them made to stand, the fire crackling between them. "I won't keep you," Theomer finally said, shifting to lean forward, "but I have to ask. Do you have a favorite of Avra's suitors?"

"Oh, Ellemere, completely. Ma likes *Byute* for some reason."

Theomer smiled. "Ellemere's mine, too. Although, I could see why your mother favors Byute."

A yawn prevented Heron from responding immediately. "Maybe we'll have to continue this discussion over breakfast?"

Theomer regarded em, head tipped back slightly, considering. "All right. If you'd like. I don't want to encroach..."

Emboldened, Heron rose and stepped up to Theomer, raising eir eyebrows as ey handed him the book. This close, ey could see just how snarled Theomer's hair was—how long it had been since it had been tended to. "Not at all. I've got to hear an opinion on Byute from someone other than Ma. Maybe you'll actually be able to explain the appeal."

Theomer took the book, looking back at em. "Then I look forward to it. Good night, Heron."

5

HERON ENJOYED BREAKFAST with Theomer the next day, and on the days that followed. Ey enjoyed the hours spent in the garden, doing mundane tasks and discovering more wonders, things like a rhododendron shrub with bright yellow blooms and a tendril of clematis that reached out and curled around eir wrist when ey knelt near it. With the overgrowth mostly cleared, ey could start actually tending to the plants now, pulling up choking weeds, trimming for aesthetic rather than utilitarian reasons. The shed held an assortment of seeds, some of which were suitable for planting now. That would be the next step, filling in the bare patches with new life.

Ey enjoyed having dinner with Theomer at the end of each day, and reading to him afterward. Ey enjoyed falling into bed each night feeling tired and satisfied. Satisfied enough that sometimes, it all felt too perfect, this respite ey'd been granted from eir normal life. Ey had to remind emself not to settle in too much. It was only temporary, and anyway, given enough time, something would inevitably go wrong. Ey'd been happy with Tiel at first, too, and look where that had gotten em.

But, for as long as it lasted, ey might as well appreciate it, right?

One evening when ey and Theomer retired to the parlor, the door on one side of the room—which, ey'd idly noted before, had to lead to the only area of the first floor ey hadn't seen—was ajar. As ey sat eir eyes darted to it, and when ey drew them away and picked up the book, Theomer said, "You can ask, you know. If you want to see it." He looked to be suppressing a smile, and Heron rolled eir eyes and tried to hold back one of eir own.

"Right, sorry. I forgot I'm allowed to be open about my nosiness. Well then—what's in there?"

"Technically it's the drawing room." Theomer rose and beckoned Heron to follow. "We always called it the music room, though." He pushed the door wide, and the lamps inside flickered to life, illuminating couches, a cold fireplace, more old-style paintings on the walls. One spot where it looked like a painting had hung, but was now gone. And in one corner, a harpsichord.

The only place Heron had seen one before was the inn, where it was played at dances and performances. "Oh—I've heard you playing. I mean, that was you, right? I'm assuming the servants don't have any hidden musical talent."

"Yes." Theomer was turned away slightly, his hair hiding his face. "I didn't realize you'd be able to hear it, out there."

"I liked it," Heron assured him. "I mean, I can't say I'm really qualified to judge, but it sounded nice. May I...?" Ey lifted a hand, wiggling eir fingers, and Theomer swept his own hand out in invitation. Heron stepped up to the instrument and plinked a few keys, eliciting random, vibrant notes. Ey wanted to hear Theomer play up close, wanted to see him sitting at the thing creating melodies, but ey wasn't about to ask for that.

"It's lovely." Ey flashed him a quick smile. "Don't hold back playing on my account."

They returned to the parlor, Theomer leaving the door to the music room cracked open behind them. And the next day as Heron worked, the strains of the harpsichord drifted out to em again, lasting longer than before.

One morning Heron woke to the spattering of rain. As ey dressed and walked down to breakfast, ey decided to start the day by re-organizing the shed; hopefully the rain would have let up by the time ey was done. If not, ey could work in it; ey'd done it before. But when ey sat down, Theomer remarked, "Looks like no gardening today."

"What, you think a little rain can stop me?" Heron raised eir eyebrows.

"It's more a matter of 'should' than 'can'. I'll leave it up to you, but just know you're under no obligation."

Heron's eyes strayed to the window, to the sheets of water pouring down. "Well. I could read you a bit of *Avra*, for now, while I wait for it to let up?"

Theomer agreed. The rain did not let up, and Heron found ey didn't mind. Ey read the entire second-to-last part of *Avra*, and when ey glanced out the window, shrugged, and asked Theomer if ey should continue, Theomer said, "Let's take a break for now," and Heron thought ey was being dismissed. Ey got to eir feet, ready to go organize the shed after all, but then Theomer said, "Oh, I meant—we could do something else? Cards, chess?"

Heron sank back into eir chair. "I've never actually played chess."

"Oh? Would you like to?"

"You know, I think I would."

They drew the chairs closer together before the fire, and an automaton produced a table with an inlaid checkerboard. A velvet-lined case held the pieces, heavy and ornate, one set silver and one bronze. Theomer arranged the silver ones on his side of the board, and Heron mirrored him on the other.

Theomer told em what all the pieces did, but ey couldn't entirely keep them straight. Ey spent much too long on each of eir turns staring at the board, not wanting to make a fool of emself, and then inevitably making a choice to which Theomer would respond something like, "Well, if you move there, that leaves your rook open..." Finally it became so absurd ey just had to laugh at emself.

"All right, tell me what's wrong with *this* move."

"That would put you in check. Which makes it illegal."

"Well, shit. What if I went here?"

"Yes, that's not bad. Although, it will let me take this pawn..."

"But then I can take your pawn."

"...and lose your knight."

"Well, fuck. Wait, the knight is the horse?"

After Theomer's eventual victory—prolonged by his gracious permission for Heron to take back eir most egregious mistakes—Heron apologized for being the worst chess opponent in history. "Well. Maybe you'll improve in your second game?" Theomer returned, quirking an eyebrow, and Heron smirked and began reassembling eir pieces.

After two more games and then lunch, served in the parlor by automatons, Heron excused emself to the washroom. The rain had let up somewhat but still persisted, accompanied by distant thunder now. Heron wasn't sure whether ey should try to get some work done; whether Theomer wanted to spend the entire day with em, or was ready for em to be off.

As ey returned down the stairs, ey caught the now-familiar sounds of the harpsichord. Eir steps slowed as ey neared the parlor door, enjoying the playful tune, not wanting to interrupt. Theomer stopped on his own, though, and when Heron continued through the parlor to the music room, ey nearly ran into Theomer coming out.

"Oh. Sorry." Theomer took a step back.

"No—I'm sorry. Um, don't stop on my account. That was nice."

"Thank you," Theomer murmured, a flush creeping over his cheeks. Heron resisted the urge to grin at the sight.

"Actually, you know what—I have an idea. One moment..." Heron retreated to grab *Avra*, then rejoined Theomer. "If you want to, that is. I was just thinking, since we're at the end and all, you could provide some dramatic accompaniment as I read?"

Theomer's brows knitted, and Heron thought he would refuse. Maybe it was a silly idea; maybe it had been too much to ask, too forward. Maybe Theomer wasn't comfortable playing in front of em. That was why ey'd suggested doing it while ey read, though, so Theomer wouldn't have to worry about scrutiny.

Theomer scratched at his beard. "I'm not sure it'll live up to your expectations..."

"No expectations. It's just for fun. If it's not working, we'll stop."

"All right." Theomer's mouth lifted into a half-smile. "Let's try it."

They settled, Heron on one of the couches, legs stretched out across it, half-turned toward Theomer, who was seated at the harpsichord. "Ready?" Theomer asked, and Heron confirmed, "Ready."

Theomer's fingers danced over the keys in a run of high to low notes, letting the final, deepest one linger. For a moment Heron was mesmerized, but then ey shook out of it and began reading the final battle.

Honestly this part sometimes bored em a bit, with all the descriptions of weapons and the various warriors Avra took down. But when Heron paused to allow Theomer the chance to punctuate the words, he always seemed to come up with something fitting, heightening the drama or subtly mocking one of the enemies with just a few notes, turning the familiar stanzas into something new.

Avra won in the end, of course, the gods she'd pledged herself to imbuing her with extra strength when all seemed lost. Heron had hopped up to pace around the room as the tension built, book in one hand while ey gestured with the other, narrating half from memory as Theomer added dramatic chords. But when her death scene arrived, eir voice dipped low and somber. Theomer dropped his hands from the keys, eyes on Heron now.

"*To the ground our hero fell, gods' power sapping mortal flesh. Avra lay, alone and spent, fading to her final rest.*" As the gods welcomed Avra's soul to their realm, her friends wept over her body, Byute cursed the gods for not saving her and Ellemere had a shrine erected in her honor, Theomer resumed playing, a few melancholy notes here and there. Heron stood near the harpsichord now, eir gaze meeting Theomer's each time ey looked up from the page. With the last line spoken, ey let the book fall shut, and Theomer closed with a final, solemn bit of melody.

A moment of stillness, of silence, and then Heron grinned at him, the spell broken. "That was great! If I didn't know otherwise, I would have thought you'd rehearsed."

"I don't know about that." Theomer ducked his head, looking down at his lap, but then he raised his eyes to Heron again. "Your dramatic performance was excellent, though." He lifted his hands to lightly applaud.

Heron rolled eir eyes, but dipped a quick bow. "Thank you, thank you. Come back tomorrow for the opening of our next show, *Woe to the Enemies of Petra*."

"I think I just might."

Heron's eyes wandered to the window. "Oh—the rain's stopped. I didn't even notice."

"You're not planning to go work now, are you? We need to talk about that ending—I wasn't expecting the gods to step in, after neglecting Avra for so long..."

So Heron stayed, and they talked till dinner, and then through it in the dining room, and afterward Theomer said he wasn't about to ask Heron to read any more, eir voice had to be tired, but would ey like a chess rematch? Heron agreed, and they played until it was dark.

When Heron stood to go to bed, after losing several more games, Theomer rose too and stood facing em. "Well, good night, Heron. And—thank you. For today."

"Oh—no need to thank me. Um, I enjoyed it. Thank *you*. Um... good night."

Ey hastened away before ey could babble anymore, unsure why Theomer's quiet gratitude made em feel like the world had tilted, and ey had to scramble to stay upright.

THREE MORNINGS LATER, Heron arrived at the dining room to find the table set as usual, but Theomer absent. Ey took eir seat dubiously, wondering what had happened to change his routine.

The last two days had been clear, and ey'd spent them back in the garden. For the first time, though, ey'd wondered what Theomer did all day—besides playing the harpsichord—and whether he enjoyed doing it. Whether he would rather have hired a companion than a gardener; if that was why he'd wanted Ma to stay over em. But ey had brushed those away as silly, pointless thoughts. Of course ey didn't know what Theomer was thinking, what he felt. What he wanted.

Heron had only been waiting at the table for a minute when Theomer walked in—clean-shaven. Ey couldn't help staring. "Yes, I know," Theomer said before ey could find words. He turned his head, letting his still-matted hair fall in front of his face. "I decided it was time I do something about... this." He waved a hand to indicate his entire head.

"Well," was all Heron could come up with at first. The beard's absence revealed the strong lines of Theomer's chin, the hint of his cheekbones. "Um, good job. Very, ah, smooth."

"Yes, well, that was the easy part." Theomer held up a hank of his hair, wincing. "This will be a bit more difficult. I... wondered if you could help me? After breakfast?"

"...All right." Heron wasn't sure exactly what that would entail—chopping it all off? It would be a shame if Theomer lost all those impressive locks, but if it was what he wanted...

They talked over last night's portion of *Petra* as they ate, but Heron was mildly distracted. Ey'd never cut anyone's hair before. What if ey left Theomer's head a mess of ragged tufts? Well, maybe they would just laugh about it together. It could hardly be worse than his hair's current state.

When the automatons brought the post-meal coffee, Theomer crooked a finger at one of them. "Prepare a basin of warm water in the washroom?" It inclined its head and departed.

Oh—Heron would be *washing* Theomer's hair. Why was that even more nerve-wracking than cutting it? Eir heart suddenly seemed to be beating too close to eir skin.

Theomer was currently speculating on whether Byute would show up in Petra's story now that Ellemere had made an appearance, and Heron refocused on the conversation, putting on an innocent smile accompanied by a shrug, not about to give the answer away. Ey swallowed eir coffee in a few gulps, though, too restless to linger over it.

"Ready?" Theomer asked after finishing his own with a long draught, eyebrows raised.

"Yes." Heron was on eir feet almost as soon as the word left eir mouth, and ey cringed internally; it would be odd to come across as *eager*.

Ey followed Theomer through the empty entrance hall and up the stairs, struggling to match his long strides until he glanced back and slowed. "Sorry. I'm not used to…"

It was strange to hear Theomer trail off, apparently having started the sentence without knowing where it would go. "It's fine," Heron answered when he didn't continue. "I *am* used to—" Ey cut emself off; ey'd meant to say *being a step behind*, but it seemed too self-deprecating, or like an insult to Theomer, which certainly wasn't what ey meant. Instead, ey just repeated, "It's fine."

The requested basin of steaming water awaited them in the washroom, alongside a pile of cushions. While Theomer unclasped his cloak, Heron fussed with arranging them, giving Theomer privacy as he partially undressed.

When Theomer turned, stepping toward em, Heron hopped to eir feet. Theomer stood with his shoulders hunched, and any measure of intimidation in his demeanor seemed to have dropped away with the cloak. He looked smaller now, more vulnerable, the cut of his loose shirt exposing the pale skin of his throat. A mere half-hour of sunlight would be enough to burn him. His only adornment was a chain around his neck, whatever hung at the end hidden beneath his shirt.

Theomer met Heron's gaze, his expression hesitant, unsure. Right. Heron had a job to do. "All right, so, if you lie down here..."

Theomer sank down to sit on the floor, then lay back, shifting a bit. Heron knelt and trailed a hand through the water as if to test the temperature, needing to do *something* while ey waited.

"All right." Theomer's eyes cut sideways to Heron for a brief moment before fluttering shut. "I'm ready." He tilted his head back, letting his hair float and then sink into the waiting water.

Heron's hands hovered over the basin for a moment. Theomer no longer being able to see em took some of the pressure off, but at the same time, it made em more nervous. Theomer was trusting em with this personal, intimate job. What if ey fucked it up somehow?

No. It was just hair, that was all. Just work, just another task to complete; another thing that needed cleaning up and sorting out. Ey immersed eir hands, fingers briefly cupping Theomer's scalp to pull his head back a little farther before delving into the thick brown mass. Ey swished the floating strands through the water, thoroughly wetting them, then set to work prising apart the smaller snarls, leaving the larger ones to soak. All the while Theomer's eyes remained shut, eyelids twitching occasionally in response to a splash or an accidental pull, which Heron muttered apologies for, to which Theomer murmured back, "It's fine."

Once enough of the hair was disentangled, ey lifted the waiting bar of lavender-scented soap and scrubbed up a lather. As ey began working it through Theomer's hair, eir eyes crept to the man's face, studying the details as his body moved slightly with each breath. Long, elegant nose; thick eyebrows; prominent jaw. Cheeks— their bareness still startling—red where the razor had irritated the unaccustomed skin. Pale, lightly chapped lips, which were slightly parted at the moment...

Ey made emself look away, retrieving the soap to lather up some more. What would Tiel think if he saw this? There was something about the cushions, Theomer's prone form, Heron kneeling over him, taking such care with the tangled strands, fingers practically caressing Theomer's scalp...

"Do you have a comb?" ey blurted, rocking back, abruptly withdrawing eir sudsy hands. "Sorry, I should have asked for that at the beginning."

"Oh." Theomer's eyes fluttered open. "Yes, of course."

Heron scrambled to eir feet, but Theomer motioned

to the automaton standing silently by the door, and it strode off into the hall. Of course. Had ey really thought Theomer would send em into his bedroom?

With a long breath in, ey knelt again, hands once more cupping Theomer's head, tilting it back a bit farther. Ey teased apart the remaining matted clumps, aided by the comb the automaton delivered. Finally eir fingers slid easily through the now-silken strands, loosing the remaining soap, and Theomer sighed. "That feels good."

Heron's motions stuttered for a moment. The words made em feel like this was more than just innocent hair-washing. Eir throat was suddenly dry, eir stomach suddenly warm...

"Having it clean, I mean," Theomer went on, eyes still closed. "I can feel the difference already."

"Oh. Right." Heron was grateful that Theomer couldn't see eir reddening face, and ey sped up eir rinsing, finishing the process with a pitcher of fresh water.

"All right. All done." Ey sat back on eir heels, and Theomer heaved himself up, twisting to kneel with his neck bent over the basin, hair dripping into it. Heron grabbed the waiting towel and thrust it into his hands, eir warm, pinkened fingers meeting Theomer's cold, pale ones.

"Thank you." Theomer shifted, sitting back and enveloping his hair in the towel, patting it down. His eyes found Heron's. "I don't think that would have gone as well with one of the servants in your place." He offered a brief smile, the towel slipping down to leave his hair free, hanging wet and stringy around his face. Why was the sight so charming?

"Ha, I bet your hair would have gotten caught in its finger joints. We'd have to name the unfortunate fucker 'hairy hands'." Heron smirked as ey got to eir feet, wiping eir own hands on eir trousers. "Um, but, you're welcome. Happy I could help."

Theomer pressed the towel against his face, absorbing a rivulet running down his forehead. "Well then, I'll see you for dinner?" he asked, voice muffled.

"Yes—of course."

It felt wrong to leave him like that, on the floor, the cushions needing to be picked up, the water needing to be disposed of. But the automatons would take care of that. Theomer didn't need em anymore.

Pulling up dead stalks and replacing them with new seeds kept Heron's hands occupied, but allowed eir mind to wander. Eir body still held a measure of tension, eir mind still holding the image of Theomer, eyes closed, putting himself in Heron's care.

Do I need to be jealous? Tiel teased in eir mind. Not serious, not really meaning it, because he didn't have any doubts that Heron remained committed to him. Why should he?

Heron scowled at a climbing hydrangea nearby. The

first time ey'd been working near it, ey'd stood to find one of its vines wrapped around eir ankle, nearly tripping em. The resistance when ey'd unwound it had been much greater than it should have been. Ey planned to find some stones to build a low wall around it, keeping future unsuspecting ankles safe.

I trust your judgment, Theomer had said, back at the beginning. Beyond the garden, the rambling forest halted at the property's encircling wall. Somehow, Heron had been allowed to breach that barrier, and then another, and another... When, seemingly, no one else had. Not for quite some time.

Of course, that was only due to a combination of happenstance and Ma's machinations. Theomer hadn't chosen em; he'd wanted it to be Ma here. She could have been the one reading to Theomer, listening to him play, washing his hair. There was nothing special about Heron.

Having finished tucking a series of columbine seeds into the dirt, ey decided it was time to haul some rocks. Hopefully ey'd end up too tired to keep having these ridiculous thoughts.

Hours later, eir shadow stretching long over the plants, the automatons putting away the tools for the day, ey pulled eir trowel from the dirt to join them. Ey caught a whiff of eir own sweat and grimaced—it had been a warmer day, and ey'd have to make sure to wash well before dinner in order to be presentable company...

"Heron?"

Ey started, falling back on eir ass, dropping the trowel, turning eir head toward the voice. Theomer was standing in the kitchen doorway.

"Sorry. I wasn't sure how to avoid startling you."

"It's fine." Heron scrambled to eir feet, standing with eir back unusually straight, struck speechless by Theomer's transformation. The shaving this morning had made quite a difference already, but now, with his hair clean... Fully dry, it had a slight wave to it, and shone amber where it caught the sun. He wore it half pulled back, unable to hide his face, the loose half draping his shoulders. A long, deep blue jacket had replaced his cloak. He looked like the hero of a classic novel, a noble lord. Except for his posture, shrinking slightly under Heron's gaze; except for his expression, uncertain, eyes cast down.

Ey wanted to say *You look good*, but those words refused to leave eir mouth. Instead, "You clean up well" emerged, sounding casual, offhand. As if ey didn't want to keep staring, didn't want to move closer and touch Theomer's hair again, to see if it was as soft as it looked. "Am I late for dinner?"

"No." Now Theomer's eyes darted up to Heron's face, his chin lifting slightly. "I just wanted to come see your progress. Would you give me a tour?"

"Oh—yes, of course."

Nerves danced through Heron as ey led Theomer around, babbling about the mundane and magical plants alike. A bit worried that eir work would be a disappointment, that ey'd failed to live up to Theomer's expectations. But Theomer nodded along, commenting once in a while. "I forgot we had those," or "I like what you've done there." He seemed perfectly happy with Heron's choices, and by the time they'd reached the fountain at the far end, Heron felt silly for being concerned.

They stopped before the empty basin, and Theomer's gaze rose to the figures at the top—the lovers, he'd called them. Heron's eyes went wide when they caught the fallen lily bloom ey'd set atop the headless one's neck—it had been a whim ey'd indulged earlier, finding the orange flower too pretty to discard, and enjoying placing something in that empty space.

"More of your work?" Theomer asked, nodding toward the flower, and Heron couldn't read his tone.

"...Yes, I just stuck it up there, I don't know, it seemed—"

Theomer silenced em with a brief touch of eir arm. "I like it."

Heron breathed out. Ey almost babbled a trite line about turning brokenness into beauty, but instead said simply, "Me too."

Theomer turned and settled on the fountain's wide rim, his back to the statue now, and Heron sat beside him. For the first time since ey'd begun work, ey took in the garden as a whole. Ey'd made good progress—it hardly looked like the same place. Still slightly wild, slightly untameable, but that was part of its charm. Part of what made it beautiful.

Theomer regarded it too before his gaze moved to Heron, body shifting along with it. "It's coming along nicely. You're good at this—tending it, I mean. Caring for it."

Heron shrugged, scooping up a stray ivy leaf from the ground to twirl between eir fingers. "It's what I've done all my life. Just, with crops instead of ornamental plants."

"I don't think it's just that, though." Now Theomer touched eir knee, lightly, just for a moment. "You have skill. But more than that, you have passion. You're invested, and it shows."

Heron's free hand twitched where it rested on eir leg, close to the spot Theomer's fingers had brushed. Ey kept eir eyes on the leaf in eir hands. "Well. Thank you. For the compliment, and the opportunity."

Those sounded almost like parting words; as if ey had finished, and was about to go on eir way. "Of course, there's still more to be done," ey continued. "That corner is still a bit of a mess, more planting to do..."

"Your mother said she's hoping to get out of farming one day, to work solely on her machines," Theomer remarked. "What will you do then?"

Heron felt Theomer's eyes on em, felt the weight of the question—of someone asking em what ey wanted.

"I'm... not entirely sure," ey admitted, glancing up at Theomer, letting the leaf fall. "Stay on and keep it up, maybe. Could switch over to cultivating flowers, now that I've gotten this experience." Ey gave a light shrug.

Theomer half-smiled; why did Heron want him to never stop? "Well. If you ever want a change, there'll always be a position open for you here."

He rose before Heron could respond, turning to offer his hand. Heron took it, feeling slightly dazed. Ey let Theomer pull em to eir feet, and then they stood facing each other, hands still clasped, the sun lighting Theomer's face and glinting off his hair. Awash in the scent of primroses—which, Heron had discovered, came from the foxgloves—with the low whine of insects in the background. Theomer's hand was larger than Heron's, his grip firm yet gentle, fingers smooth against Heron's calloused ones. No sign that he noticed or cared about the dirt coating them.

"Dinner?" Heron asked, the word coming out raspy.

"Dinner," Theomer agreed, and dropped Heron's hand. Why, as he turned toward the castle, did ey ache for him to grasp it again?

IN THE GARDEN THE NEXT DAY, strains of one of the quick, cheerful melodies Theomer was favoring lately drifting out to em, Heron couldn't stop his words from echoing in eir mind.

A position open for you...

Why did eir heart leap every time ey recalled them? It wasn't because ey loved the garden—not that much. The notion of bringing some seeds and cuttings home to start eir own flower garden was exciting too. But... staying here... with Theomer...

Last night when they'd gone to read, Theomer had ventured into the music room and sat down at the harpsichord, playing a brief tune; when he'd caught Heron staring at his hands, he'd smiled and said, "Here, sit," sliding over to make room. And when Heron had, barely an inch between their bodies, Theomer had guided eir hand into position on the keys. "All right, now press down with this finger, this finger, and this finger."

Heron had, producing a simple chord. "Hmm. Not so hard after all," ey'd quipped, while unable to keep the grin off eir face. Theomer's mouth had quirked up in response, and then he'd placed his hand over Heron's again, playing a simple tune through Heron's fingers, making Heron's breath catch in eir throat. Ey'd longed to shift eir fingers to entwine with Theomer's; ey'd longed to run eir other hand through Theomer's thick, luxurious hair. Ey'd longed—

Ey clenched eir teeth against the memory. It was foolish. This was all a silly fancy born of eir unhappiness with Tiel. Ey'd gotten swept away in the thrill of meeting someone new; these feelings weren't real, they didn't mean anything. Theomer was still largely a mystery, and ey had no reason to think he'd made that offer for any reason beyond appreciating Heron's gardening abilities.

But—why did that hardly seem to matter? Why did even the prospect of merely continuing their simple routine, nothing changing between them, seem so preferable to returning to eir old life?

That afternoon the message-carrier returned, the one Heron had sent to Ma... when had that been? Days, weeks...? Time had run together such that it could have been two months, or only a fortnight.

Ey unrolled the paper anticipating a chatty update about Ma's machine, the farm, how she missed em.

Except it wasn't from Ma at all.

Heron, my love—

I was hoping I would have heard from you again by now, perhaps with news of when you'll be returning? Your mum told me you've been paid already, and surely by now you've done enough to earn it? I just talked to her about our plan, and she said it's fine, you're free to do whatever you like. So please, come back so that we can finally begin our new life together!

XX, Tiel

Ey stared at the words, hand tightening on the paper until it crumpled. Tiel had talked to Ma *for* em? What, he'd gotten tired of waiting for Heron, and just decided to do it himself? So that *his* plan could proceed, on *his* schedule, exactly the way *he* wanted?

Eir gaze went to the fountain, where ey and Theomer had sat last night. Abandoning the seeds ey'd been planting, ey crossed the garden and got to work neatening the area around it. Ey plucked dead blossoms from the surrounding plants, trimmed the flanking boxwoods into symmetry, and replaced the statue's lily, which had fallen into the basin. By the time ey finished, by the time ey stepped back to admire eir work, ey had banished all eir hesitation and uncertainty. Ey knew what ey wanted, and more importantly in this moment, ey knew what ey *didn't* want. It was time Tiel knew as well.

"How do I get the water running?" ey asked the

automaton who'd been scooping the boxwood trimmings into a wheelbarrow. It straightened up and led em out of the garden, around the wall to the area behind the fountain—to a rusted wheel set in a stone in the ground, nearly hidden by the tall grasses around it. It took several tries, leaving Heron panting, but ey eventually got it to turn with a screech, and moments later, heard the gratifying sound of splashing water.

Ey hopped the wall, careful not to squash any plants, and stood before the fountain again. It was lovely, the water overflowing each basin to spill into the next, the lovers' reflection rippling against the base's blue tile. The water came from their joined hands, as if created by their bond. Okay, that was sappy. But—seeing it was nice. The way it was meant to be, aside from one flower-instead-of-head.

Ey stuck a hand in the frigid stream, letting it chill eir fingers for a moment, then turned away. Time for dinner. Time to make eir announcement.

"So," Heron said after they'd settled into their meal, vegetable dumplings with a side of spiced rice tonight, "I was thinking I should go home for a visit. Just a short one, to check in on Ma, see if she needs anything..."

Ey was going to tell Theomer about Tiel—later, after it was over. Ey would confess the whole thing, pour it out alongside eir other confession.

"Oh." Theomer seemed caught off guard, but went

on, "Yes, that's reasonable. When were you planning to go?"

"Tomorrow? If that's okay, if it's not too soon…" Heron felt a bit awkward, apologetic, as if ey were abandoning Theomer; as if it were a betrayal, somehow, to leave him to go see Tiel. As if Tiel wasn't the one actually being betrayed.

But no, that wasn't fair. Ey had stayed committed to Tiel through all of eir discontent and unhappiness, and now that ey was finally ready to be done, ey was going to go tell him so. It wasn't a betrayal to be honest.

"Yes, that's fine," Theomer answered. "You can take my carriage."

"Oh, good—thank you."

Theomer nodded, and then silence stretched between them until he made a remark about *Petra*, and they got to talking about the book again. Over their post-dinner tea, though, Theomer fell silent, staring down into his cup. "Listen," he said finally, lifting his head, drawing Heron's full attention. "Before you go… there's something I want to show you."

Heron's heart was not suddenly pounding double-time; ey did not want to immediately scramble to eir feet, ready to follow Theomer anywhere. "All right." Ey met Theomer's gaze, matching his solemnity, adding a quick nod.

Theomer swallowed the rest of his tea and rose. Heron followed him out into the main hall, up the stairs to the second floor. Theomer kept his stride measured, but Heron still hung back a step. Were they—going to Theomer's room?

But no, Theomer led em to the third floor, across the sun-bathed workshop, to the turret door.

"I know I told you it's not safe in here," he said without turning around. "It's true, just... not in the way you'd expect." The door creaked as he pulled it open. "You'll see."

Heron certainly had questions, but eir trust in Theomer kept them in check. Ey followed him through the doorway. Inside, a stone staircase spiraled upward. Mustiness hung in the air. Narrow, diamond-paned windows cast a stark pattern of light and shadow as they climbed. The only sound was the scuff of shoes on stone.

At the top, another door waited. Theomer lifted the chain that hung around his neck, revealing a key at the end. The lock turned with a squeal of disuse, and Theomer pushed the door wide.

For a moment he stood still, blocking Heron's view, but when he stepped aside, eir mouth curved into a silent O. Serrated leaves covered every surface of the round room, stalks of some sort of plant having wended their way over the bookshelves lining the walls, across the window seats, and even the windows themselves, creating a lattice of shadows in the sinking sun's golden light. A desk had become a trellis; the floor was almost entirely hidden beneath the foliage. It was the castle's library, but also a miniature, indoor garden.

Heron let out a puff of breath, half incredulous, half marveling. "Gods. It's beautiful."

Theomer's hand brushed eirs, and Heron glanced at him. "Look closer," he said softly. Frowning, Heron turned to the nearest bookcase, where a sunbeam lit one of the vines that had crawled across the spines—a vine studded with curved red thorns.

The plants were overgrown rose stalks, no flowers in sight but, now that ey was looking for them, thorns everywhere. Like a lovely dream turned nightmare.

"What *is* this?" ey hissed, spinning to face Theomer, wide-eyed, aghast. The plant wasn't a pretty embellishment; it had ruined the place, making it unusable, the books nearly inaccessible.

"It's... the reason I'm here." Theomer stepped up to Heron's side, crushing stems beneath his feet. "Look there." He nodded toward the desk, and Heron approached it slowly. A shape sat beneath the tangle, outlined by the innumerable stalks flowing out of it. A vase?

Ey leaned in, haltingly, as if whatever was inside might be waiting to pounce. At the bottom sat a single large rose blossom. Deep red, nearly black, lurking among the stems like a spider in a web. Wafting a sour scent, like rot, or death. As ey stared, a shiver passed over the petals, as if the thing were aware of eir gaze.

Drawing back, Heron turned to Theomer. "The plants in the garden..."

Theomer let out a long sigh. "They weren't *meant* to

be preparation for this, but..."

During his several beats of silence, Heron nearly succumbed to the temptation to look behind em and check that the cursed flower hadn't left its lair. But instead ey watched Theomer, waiting for him to be ready to continue.

"It keeps me on the estate." The words tumbled from Theomer's mouth in an uncharacteristic rush. "I'm bound to it."

Before Heron could ask any questions, Theomer shrugged off his jacket, letting it fall to the floor, and rolled one of his sleeves up to the elbow. Heron's breath hissed in through eir teeth. A piece of a rose stem, several inches long, was embedded beneath the translucent surface of Theomer's skin, paralleling the long vein in his forearm. A white scar at one end marred his flesh. Before Heron's horrified gaze, a new thorn emerged from the stalk and pierced through the skin, sending a bead of blood rolling down Theomer's arm.

"Fuck," ey breathed. "Theomer—" Ey whirled around to take in the room again, ready to run to the garden shed for shears, or start tearing the monstrous plant out with eir bare hands.

"Wait." Theomer touched eir arm again, and Heron went still, meeting his eyes. "I want... to explain."

Theomer was so calm, lacking anything like desperation. He hadn't brought Heron here to solve this problem, had he, but simply to hear his story. Ey swallowed, and nodded, and tried to release some of the tension animating eir body. "All right."

"Well, as I've indicated, I grew up here." Theomer's gaze dropped to his still-bared arm. "I was an orphan, and the mages took me in, as a companion for their son. They found this place, or inherited it, I don't remember. But they made it their own, somewhere they could work on their mechanical experiments.

"Their son turned out to have more of an aptitude for plant magic, so they let him work in the garden. I tended it, and gave him advice and ideas about using magic on the plants. We... became lovers, when we were older. But—his parents died in some sort of accident. Neither of us knew exactly what happened, but it scared him. He thought something might happen to us. I told him we should leave, that we would be safest if we got away from here, but he became obsessed with creating a protection spell. He thought he could use the plants, but when he tried... it became this."

Theomer punctuated the words with a slight shrug. "It wasn't his fault; the magic was just too powerful, and he lost control. The spell was twisted into something to keep one prisoner, instead of keeping one safe. It... took me first, and..." He trailed off, thumb tracing the line of the plant in his arm. "Well, when he realized, he was afraid. He fled. I've... been here alone ever since."

Horror and fury burned through Heron, making eir teeth clench. Ey would tear that man apart if ey could. How dare he be so cowardly, so cruel, as to abandon Theomer to this fate instead of doing all he could to free him.

"There has to be a way to destroy it." Heron's gaze fixed on the vase again, then shifted to the stalks covering the room. "Rip it out, burn it…"

In answer, Theomer stepped up to the desk and reached for one of the stems spilling from the vase. It writhed in his grasp, coming to sudden, violent life, but he held on and snapped it in two. The loose end immediately wrapped around his hand, thorns digging into his flesh, while the one attached to the rose flailed in the air. Heron leapt forward, ready to rescue Theomer if need be, but when he plucked the one off his hand, the severed ends met and knitted themselves back together. Theomer took a step back, and the plant fell still again.

"I've tried." With a soft sigh, he turned away. "I'm resigned to it, now."

"Theomer." Heron's voice cracked as ey stepped in front of him, anger melting into grief. Ey lay a hand on his arm and looked up at him until Theomer looked back. "You shouldn't have to resign yourself. You don't deserve this." Eir hand rose to Theomer's beardless cheek; Theomer twitched slightly, but didn't pull away. Head tilted back to meet his eyes, gaze unwavering, Heron whispered fiercely, "He didn't deserve you."

Emotion flickered across Theomer's face as he stood frozen for a long moment. Heron was about to drop eir hand and draw back, mumbling an apology—ey'd gotten carried away; this wasn't what ey'd planned, it wasn't what Theomer wanted—

But then Theomer's hands were on eir waist, pulling em closer, and Theomer's lips were meeting eirs. Warm and soft, sending flowers bursting into bloom in Heron's chest. Eir eyes fell shut and ey slid eir hand to the back of Theomer's neck, weaving into his hair, holding on as eir mouth opened to welcome his. Eir body sang at his touch, and ey was ready to drop to the floor with him, thorns be damned. This—wanting someone, and being wanted back, not just physically but as an entire person, being seen and known by someone who wanted to see and know more—

"Mmm—" Eir mouth broke free so ey could gasp in a breath. And suddenly the rest of the world fell back into place. Ey was here, in this room, in this... situation, because ey was leaving tomorrow. Leaving to tell Tiel goodbye.

Part of em whispered, *Fuck Tiel*. It would be so easy to forget about him and his assumptions and his wishes, to just give in to what *ey* wanted in this moment. To what Theomer clearly wanted, too.

But—there were things ey owed Tiel first. The truth, at least, and an honest goodbye, before Heron committed emself to someone else.

Another obstacle held em back as well—Theomer didn't know about Tiel. And while theoretically ey didn't have to tell him, could simply brush Tiel away as something in the past that Theomer never needed to learn of, Heron didn't *want* to lie to him, didn't want to hide. Ey wanted to open emself up and show Theomer everything—because Theomer, of all people, would want to see it. Would accept it, without judgment.

Theomer's breath tickled eir face; he still held Heron close. When eir eyes met his, he smiled and leaned in again.

Internally cursing emself, Heron pulled back slightly. "Wait."

Theomer drew away immediately, hands dropping from Heron's sides. "I'm sorry. I thought—"

"Oh, no—you thought correctly. *Gods*, don't doubt that. It's just..." Heron's eyes darted around the room, searching for something, anything to light on that wasn't Theomer's face. They finally settled on a stalk that had curled around a ceiling beam, wrapping it in a painful embrace. "I have—someone. At home. A... lover."

In the corner of eir eye, Theomer didn't move, didn't say anything. Heron couldn't make emself face him. "But the reason I'm going back is to tell him I'm done," ey rushed on. "I haven't been happy with him for a long time—that was why I wanted to stay here, to get away and have time to decide what I was going to do. Even though, really, I knew all along what it should be, it just... took me a while to find the fucking backbone to tell him. But now I'm ready, and that's partly because..."

Finally, eir gaze moved to Theomer's. He remained still, impassive, cheeks slightly pink, lips darkened with the flush Heron's had given them. Heron's eyes dropped to the floor. Ey wished ey were barefoot among the thorns; it would have been a fitting penance. "Because I want you," ey finished, the words rasping out in a whisper.

The ensuing silence seemed to stretch on into eternity. Until— "You never mentioned him." Theomer's voice was calm, even, as if he were making a casual observation. As if the fact were unimportant, instead of something that was opening up a chasm between them.

"I know," Heron mumbled, overtaken by shame. "I should have, and I'm sorry I didn't. But—I'm telling you now."

Ey couldn't help eir voice lifting with hope. Ey looked back at Theomer, but he wasn't looking at em. He stared off at the plant-covered west window, where the last of the sun's rays were slowly disappearing.

"I need—some time." When Theomer spoke, Heron heard the words as if from far away. "You should keep to your plan, go home tomorrow and do what you need to do. If I decide I want more work done on the garden, I'll send for you."

Heron's mouth was dry, eir chest tight. Was this it, then? All the hours they'd spent together, the moments they'd shared, the feelings inside em desperate to burst free... Had ey really ruined all of it?

"Theomer..."

Theomer's hand jolted upward in a "halt" motion, which Heron heeded, words dying on eir tongue.

"Heron. Please. Go."

Each word felt like a knife to eir heart. Ey closed eir eyes. "...All right." When ey opened them, Theomer remained facing away. "I'll go."

As ey finally made eir feet move, finally stepped out the door, ey was wrenched with longing to look back. This was eir last chance to see Theomer's face; the last chance for Theomer to ask em to wait, to say he'd hear em out. To say he didn't want Heron to leave like this.

But—if Heron looked, and Theomer didn't...

Ey swallowed and kept walking, gaze remaining fixed straight ahead.

HERON'S SLEEP WAS RACKED with dreams—of Theomer appearing at eir door, sitting down at the end of eir bed, looking em full in the face and asking to talk. Ey kept startling awake to listen for footsteps, the sound of a knock. But every time, the castle was as eerily quiet as ever.

When dawn finally broke, ey slid from the bed. Ey'd packed eir few belongings the night before, and had meant to slip away without eating, as a sort of self-punishment. But when ey got back from the washroom, an automaton had already brought a tray of breakfast. As if to ensure ey wouldn't venture down to the dining room.

Nothing stirred in the castle as ey made eir way through it for what was, quite possibly, the last time. Out front, amidst the early-morning fog that was already burning away, a carriage waited—old-fashioned, overly decorated, and hitched to a gold, horse-like mechanical beast. All set to whisk em away.

Ey stared at it until eir eyes unfocused. Was ey really leaving? Were eir feet really carrying em forward; was ey really climbing in, settling on the padded seat, and pulling the door shut? Was the beast really towing em over the winding road down the hill, through the gate that an automaton had helpfully opened?

The answer to all of it was yes. By the time Heron truly comprehended that, the castle was out of sight.

The carriage stopped near the edge of the forest—whether because the creature didn't know where to go from there, or it had the sense not to put itself on display out in the open, Heron wasn't sure, but ey was glad to get out and stretch eir legs. Behind em, the thing ponderously turned and retreated back the way it had come. Ey stood watching it for too long—eir last connection to Theomer, slowly disappearing from view.

The sun's heat was cushioned away behind a layer of clouds, and a pleasant breeze caressed eir face as ey reached eir yard, where the chickens pecked about, carefree as ever. Two fluttered their wings and hopped away when ey swung emself over the fence, but the smallest, eir favorite, waddled up to em, and ey scooped her up and held her against eir chest for a long moment.

Iggy stuck her head out of the barn; ey waved at her,

and she waved back before withdrawing. Good to know the farm work was getting done, at least.

The main room of the house was in a bit of disarray, chicken feathers and dried grass scattered across the floor, dishes piled in the sink. "Ma?" ey called.

"Heron?" A moment later she hobbled out of her bedroom, which doubled as her workshop, puzzled face softening into a grin as she wrapped em in a hug. "You should've sent word you were coming! I would have gone to the market and gotten something special for dinner."

"Sorry, I didn't think to. I only just decided to come yesterday."

"Oh?" She tilted her head as she regarded em. "Did something happen?"

"Not... exactly..." Simple was best for now. "I need to talk to Tiel."

"Ah." Understanding bloomed on her face, but fortunately, she didn't ask for more.

"I'll go after dinner."

"Good, so you'll spend some time with your old ma in the meantime? I want to hear all about what it's been like, what you've been doing, what you've learned about our mysterious host..."

"I should see if Iggy needs any help—"

"Oh, she's got it taken care of. You sit down and let yourself rest for once."

Heron complied without further argument, settling into eir usual chair while Ma got back to work on her machine, which as far as Heron could tell looked almost fully repaired. Ey told her about the garden, the automatons' assistance, learning chess, reading *Avra* and *Petra*. "I'd forgotten the part where Petra threatens the king, I'm not sure how I managed that..."

"Heron."

Ey looked up from the loose shirt thread ey'd been twisting around eir finger. Ma's hands were still, her gaze on em. "You've barely said his name. What is it?"

Heron's eyes squeezed shut. Ey hated emself for being so transparent. "I—" ey finally managed through gritted teeth, "developed—feelings for him. And I was a fucking fool, thinking there could be anything between us. Thinking I could..." Ey didn't even know what ey meant to say, the words drowning in a well of misery.

"He rejected you?" Ma asked gently.

Heron pulled on the thread until it snapped. "Essentially, yes. Once I confessed to being a lying slut."

"Heron."

Ey sighed; it came out huffy and childish. "I didn't tell him about Tiel. I let him think..." Ey spread eir hands helplessly. "I mean, I told him eventually, but only *after* I kissed him. Because I was fucking selfish enough to think it wouldn't matter as long as I went back and ended things with Tiel. Because I was too much of a coward to say anything to Tiel before."

"Herry." Fuck, ey hated that nickname, but when eir eyes slid up to meet Ma's, she was looking at em with tenderness, concern. "This is rather a mess you've gotten yourself into, but I don't think it's *hopeless*."

Ey just lifted eir shoulders in a long shrug. "Doesn't really matter if I have hope or not. He said not to come back unless he sends for me."

She pursed her lips, then opened her mouth again, but ey cut her off. "Please, can we not talk about it anymore? We got the money, and that was the important thing, right?"

She frowned at em, blowing out a long breath. But finally, she simply said, "Well. If you wanted something to do, the garden could use weeding..."

When Heron arrived at Tiel's door, the clouds had cleared enough to let the sun shine free on the horizon, splashing them with glorious colors. It only reminded em of last night, standing in the library, Theomer's face half light, half shadow.

Moments after ey knocked, Tiel's father opened the door. "Oh, it's you. Tiel!" he shouted before Heron could greet him. He stepped away, leaving Heron standing in the doorway.

"What?" came Tiel's voice, coated in irritation.

"Visitor."

"Who is it?" Tiel strode into view, face shifting from annoyance to joy when their eyes met. "Heron! You're back!" He reached out to clasp Heron's hand and pull em inside. "You got my letter, then?"

Heron clicked eir tongue. "I... did."

"Come on." Tiel tugged em toward the stairs and trotted up two at a time; Heron followed more slowly. "Mum's holed up with a headache," Tiel muttered, jutting his chin toward the closed door of his parents' room. "She and Da aren't speaking at the moment." Once inside his room, with the door shut behind them, he let out a sigh. "I'm so glad you're here."

The room was the same as ever, bed rumpled, clothing strewn about. Not long ago, some of it might've been Heron's.

Ey turned to Tiel, opening eir mouth to say the things ey'd planned. But then Tiel was cupping eir face in his hands and leaning in to kiss em. Heron might have let him, coward that ey was, but for the memory of Theomer's lips on eirs last night. Ey pulled away, hands catching Tiel's wrists to lower them.

"What?" Tiel half-laughed as he searched Heron's face. "Do I have foul breath?"

"No, it's not that. Tiel..."

Why was it so hard to say the words? To say *Your perception of our relationship is entirely different from mine; I know you want this, but I don't; my frustration with you has been festering for ages and it's time I finally let it go. By letting you go.* It felt like confessing to a lie, as if ey'd been deliberately fooling Tiel all this time. Apparently ey was deceiving everyone these days—including emself. Ey was the one who deserved to be shut up in an old castle, never allowed to speak to another living person...

"What is it?" Tiel asked again, and finally, Heron went on.

"I'm not—going to get rooms with you in town." Well, it was a start.

"What? Why not? Did your mum have an objection after all? She said it was fine when I talked to her—"

"No, it's not her. Tiel—you never asked whether *I* wanted to. It was all your idea, your plan."

"So then, what, you want me to come live on the farm with you?"

Heron winced. "No. I don't want us to live together at all. I—don't want us to *be* together anymore."

"What the *fuck*, Heron?" Tiel looked absolutely affronted, which was, perhaps, fair. "You come back after vanishing into the forest for weeks to tell me *this*? Did he enchant you after all? What, made you fall in love with him?" Heron's face warmed in spite of emself, and Tiel's eyes widened. "Gods, I'm *right!* Well, snap out of it!" He clapped his hands onto Heron's shoulders, giving em a shake. "It isn't real, he's manipulating you."

Heron pushed Tiel's arms away and took a step back. "For gods' sakes, Tiel, that isn't true. Do you really believe I can't think for myself at all? First I'm supposed to blithely go along with whatever it is you want, and then when I won't, the only possible explanation is that I've been ensorcelled?"

"But then where is this coming from? All of sudden you're done with me, with no warning, no good explanation—"

"*This* is the explanation right here! I never brought it up before because I knew you wouldn't fucking listen!"

Tiel started to speak, but Heron went on. "You never have, from the very start. You don't take any of my concerns seriously, you don't even pretend to be interested in anything I care about—"

"Come *on*, Heron, this isn't you."

"This *is* me! You've just never fucking paid attention!"

Tiel folded his arms, glaring, and Heron glared back.

"Fine. Just go then," Tiel finally said, turning on his heel to face the window. "Go back to your magic castle and your fake, fairytale life. Live under his spell forever for all I care."

The words continued to sting long after Heron departed. Not least because their directive wasn't actually an option; not least because they reminded Heron of the last person who had sent em away.

WAKING IN THE MORNING and scattering feed to the chickens, just like ey'd used to, felt surreal. Right back to eir old routine, eir old life. Minus Tiel. That was a relief, at least. Ey could hardly believe ey'd finally done it, and part of em was still waiting to be overtaken by regret. But on the whole, ey welcomed the change.

It was just, gazing into the future, and seeing only this—emself, Ma, the farm; endless days the same, the same, the same... When, for a brief sliver of time, ey'd looked forward to something more.

Ey didn't let emself recall that future now. Ey would be fine. Never mind that the longing in eir chest was a living thing; if ey could reach inside and pull it out to cradle in eir hands, it would pulse with its own beating heart. As long as ey didn't feed it, it would die eventually. Starved away to nothing but a ghost.

The work was a good distraction; Iggy had the

regular chores handled, and Heron didn't want to put her out of a job earlier than she'd been expecting, but ey threw emself into tackling various overdue tasks. Mending some broken planks on the barn, repainting the weathered wood in the same old red—wearing emself out so that ey would fall into bed and sleep dreamlessly. In the interim time of late afternoon, ey flopped onto Ma's bed and read to her, or really to emself, focusing on the cadence of the words and firmly not remembering the last time ey'd done this. The last person ey'd done it for.

Days passed. Tiel didn't try to contact em; nor did anyone else. Ma's machine was nearly ready now, the last vestige of the whole ordeal soon to be gone.

They were eating dinner together one night—a rare occasion when Heron had managed to pry Ma away from her work to join em at the table—when something struck one of the front windows. Heron jolted into alertness, realizing with a twinge of guilt that ey hadn't been listening to whatever Ma was saying. As ey looked up, the noise came again. Metallic, ey recognized now, and something was hovering in the air—

Ey sprang up so fast eir chair overturned. As Ma exclaimed behind em, ey flung open the door, and one of Theomer's messenger gadgets zipped up to em. Ey plucked it from the air, nearly dropping it as ey fumbled the cylinder open. Only to find it empty.

"What..." Ma started, standing at eir shoulder now, but the little machine interrupted her by springing to life again. It lifted into the air to flutter before Heron, bobbing up and down, then flew away a few feet and stopped again—waiting.

"*Fuck.*" Heron darted after it, then turned back to face a baffled-looking Ma. "Something's wrong. I have to go to him. Now."

The sun was nearly gone when Heron reached Theomer's estate, the almost-full moon brightening in its stead. Poor Old Pete wasn't used to being ridden, but he'd taken it in stride. When Heron halted before the gate, considering how best ey could scale the wall, something moved on the other side—an automaton, unlocking the gate and pulling it wide with a creak.

"Thank you," Heron called as ey spurred Pete on, up the hill, which seemed to have doubled in height. "I'm sorry, I'm sorry," ey muttered, giving the horse's neck a pat.

Ey hopped off Pete's back as soon as they reached the top. The castle remained silent and still, a shadowy, forbidding form looming above em, no lights shining from its windows. Ey flung the door open, then had to stop in the entry hall to let eir eyes adjust, just as ey had on that first day. No lights flickered on in response to eir presence.

Again something moved, and ey glanced to the side to see a row of automatons lined up against the wall. "Where...?" ey asked, even though ey had a fairly good idea. When they turned as one to point in the direction of the turret, ey took off up the stairs.

"Theomer?" Ey sprinted across the workshop, now bathed in twilight blue. There was no answer. Ey burst through the turret door and tripped running up the spiral staircase, falling hard on eir palms against the unforgiving stone, but immediately scrambled up and kept going.

The door at the top stood ajar. The room was dim, too dim; the setting sun's rays should have reached here, but the rose plant had grown at an unnatural rate, covering the windows so that only slivers of light pierced the gloom.

Heron stumbled in, nearly falling again as the thorns tangled eir feet. There, on the floor in the center—Theomer. Wrapped in his old cloak, curled on his side, his back to the door. Hair a nest around his head and shoulders, snagged by the thorns.

"Theomer!" Heron lunged forward and dropped to eir knees—thorns be damned. Eir hands hovered over Theomer's body, unsure if eir touch would be welcome.

"Heron." Theomer stirred, head turning, eyes blinking open. "I wasn't sure..."

"What—that I'd come back?" Heron half laughed, half sobbed. "I was so worried, and with good reason, fuck..."

"I'm glad the messenger reached you. When I got caught here, I didn't know if..."

"What *happened*?"

Theomer sighed, soft and resigned. "I tried again to destroy it. I wanted... to come see you. To see your home, and to tell you..." His eyes fell shut again, briefly. When they opened, he shook his head slightly. "I should have known it wouldn't let me go."

He shifted onto his back and pulled his cloak aside, uncovering his right arm. The stalk implanted there had grown, bursting out of his skin to vanish into the tangle around him. Higher up, a different stem had climbed his bicep and dug in, stabbing through his shirt, leaving a red-ringed hole in its wake. Before Heron's horrified eyes, another extended from the mass and crept to Theomer's hand, biting into his flesh and wriggling until it was partway inside his palm. Theomer's hand twitched, but otherwise he didn't react.

Heron shook emself and swatted away a stalk that was crawling toward Theomer's face. "Fuck! Come on, get up, we can break these off—"

Except the plant had wrapped Theomer's legs as well, stabbing holes through his trousers, pinning him to the floor. The one Heron had just struck was already creeping back; ey lunged forward to grab it, clamping eir fist around the end, but the thing writhed against eir hand, thorns stabbing eir palm. Finally it burst out between eir fingers, shooting forward to embed itself in Theomer's cheek.

Ey let out a growl of desperate rage, but when Theomer said, "Heron," ey stopped, staring down at him. His tone was gentle, comforting, as if Heron were the one being slowly devoured by a living rosebush. "It's too late. I knew when I sent for you. I just—wanted to see you, one more time. I wanted you to know... how happy I was. With you."

His eyes drifted shut before Heron could answer, before ey could fish words from the torrent of emotions roiling through em, before ey could choke back eir tears. "Theomer—"

Theomer didn't respond. His face was paler than normal, his lips tinging blue. Heron stared for another long moment, then scrambled to eir feet. "*No.*" It couldn't end like this. This evil magic couldn't win, Theomer's cowardly former lover couldn't win, Heron's own foolishness couldn't win—

Ey would never be able to hack this thing to pieces before it could regrow, and there was no way to burn it without also burning Theomer. Attacking it in any way would likely only get em ensnared as well. But fuck, ey was going to try—even if the result was a slow death at Theomer's side.

Ey stumbled toward the desk, which had practically vanished beneath the shroud of leaves. The form of the vase remained atop it, sheltering the rose—the plant's metaphorical, if not literal, root. Maybe, if ey could destroy it...

When ey leaned over the vase, the crimson bloom leered back at em, petals rippling. "Fuck you," ey declared, and grabbed for it.

Ey wasn't fast enough. The surrounding stems

swarmed up to block eir way, and ey flinched back, ready for them to try to delve into eir flesh. But they remained where they were, curled over the bloom. Maybe the plant didn't want to—couldn't?—hurt anyone but Theomer. Maybe ey still had a chance.

The thing's defensive maneuver had left the sides of the vase exposed. Heron yanked off eir shoe and lunged forward to smash it against the glass, striking again when it didn't break the first time. The glass crunched, and the plant writhed, moving to block the assault. Heron switched to hit the other side, shouting wordlessly, and with two more blows the vase fell away in pieces.

The barrier gone, ey plunged eir hands into the mass of flailing stems, bending and snapping, getting sliced on the thorns, until eir fingers closed around the flower. Gripping it tight enough to crush the petals, ey bent eir knees and pulled.

It resisted, and the stems thrashed toward em, wrapping themselves around eir arms—maybe ey had been wrong; maybe ey would become its second victim after all. But ey tugged harder, leaning back, putting eir full weight into the effort.

"Let—him—fucking—go!"

Ey held on through the pain as the stalks dug into eir skin, pouring all eir fear and anger into destroying the monstrous thing that had dared to hurt Theomer. And finally, with a wet, tearing sound, the rose broke free.

Later Heron remembered falling, momentum sending em flailing backwards as the stems suddenly released em, one hand flinging out while the other still clutched the rose. Cringing in anticipation of hitting the carpet of thorns—but the pain never came. Bright light assaulted eir eyes; ey didn't know whether ey was still falling, or had fallen, or had stopped in midair.

When eir eyes opened—when had they closed?—ey found emself lying on eir back, staring up at sturdy wooden ceiling beams, lit by a soft white glow. The moon was bright in the sky outside, shining in through one of the windows.

Ey shoved emself upright, gaze darting around the room. It was a cozy turret library, curved bookcases lining the walls, cushioned window seats offering an invitation to settle in and read. Not a single stalk or thorn remained. The only thing on the desk was a scatter of thick glass shards.

"Heron?" Theomer lay beside em. Blood still marred his skin and clothes, matching Heron's own sleeves and hands, but the plants had vanished from him as well.

"You're all right." Relief swelled in Heron's chest. Ey bent to examine Theomer's arm; only a purple-red bruise remained. With a grateful sigh, ey brushed some of the tangled hair back from Theomer's face, which had already regained some of its color, and used eir sleeve to dab at the wound on his cheek.

Eir other hand was still clenched tight. Uncurling eir fingers revealed a dull, dried-up rose blossom, petals already crumbling away.

When eir eyes returned to Theomer, he was looking back at em with undeniable affection. His hand lifted, brushing across Heron's cheek. "You saved me."

"Don't thank me." Shame sent Heron's gaze to the floor, whose wood gleamed as if it had been polished yesterday. Eir forgotten shoe lay upon it nearby. "It's my fault this happened. If I had just told you about Tiel at the beginning... I'm sorry I didn't. I hate that I hurt you."

Theomer pushed himself up, drawing Heron's eyes back to his face. "Heron..." he murmured. "I forgave you as soon as I woke up and remembered you weren't here anymore."

Heron let out a shaky breath, then leaned in to press eir face to Theomer's shoulder. One of Theomer's hands rose to rest, large and solid, on eir back.

"I told him," Heron said into Theomer's cloak, the scent of lavender soap filling eir nostrils. "I'm all yours now, if..."

Theomer's hand moved to eir shoulder, easing em back, and Heron lifted eir head. They sat looking at each other; Theomer was bestubbled and disheveled, bloodied and bleary-eyed, and yet still absolutely beautiful.

"Yes," he whispered, and the longing in Heron's chest burst free and took wing. Ey leaned in, and as their lips met, ey let the rose drop from eir hand. 🌹

ACKNOWLEDGMENTS

Starting from when I wrote the first draft in summer 2020, I've had so much support for this little book and have appreciated every bit of it! In roughly chronological order, my thanks to...

Ray—you told me "Heron" worked as a character name, and I am glad because now I can't imagine any other. Cécil—you talked through so many of my Tiel (and other) issues with me, read multiple early drafts, and provided so much encouragement; this book would not exist without you! Kit—you helped with plants and, after reading one of the drafts in a day, provided some much-needed affirmation. Also a shoutout to Saffron & Monica for general support during the long initial editing process. <3

Erin, Atlas, and Bennett—y'all beta read when I'd only just met you, and your feedback was both encouraging and helpful! A particular thanks to Bennett for the push to extend the hair-washing scene.

Juni, Wynn, and Talli, betas of the final version—I hadn't even met you all when I wrote the first draft, but I am so glad I have now. Your investment in the story and love for the characters (or hatred, as appropriate lol) gave me the confidence I needed to declare that DSHTPS was, at long last, done! Talli—thank you for a little extra automaton-related worldbuilding. Juni— thank you for inspiring me to write a slightly more sinister rosebush and a more dramatic ending struggle. Wynn—I will treasure your drawing of Theomer forever.

Finally, to all of Queer Lodgings—you are all excellent people whose commiseration, jokes, and enthusiasm helped me get through my final rounds of edits. You're also super smart and thoughtful, and random convos that we had helped to shape the final version of this story. Thank you for being awesome.

ABOUT THE AUTHOR

Tabitha O'Connell is a historic preservationist and writer of queer fiction living in Western New York. Eir favorite things include animals, abandoned places, alliteration, long walks, and long sentences (some of which may or may not turn up in eir work...). Right now ey is probably drinking tea and daydreaming about stories centering ace, trans, and other queer characters.

Keep up with em via...

- Website: tabithaoconnell.com
- Twitter: @tabithawrites
- Instagram: @tabitha.writes
- Newsletter: tabithaoconnell.com/newsletter